TAKEN

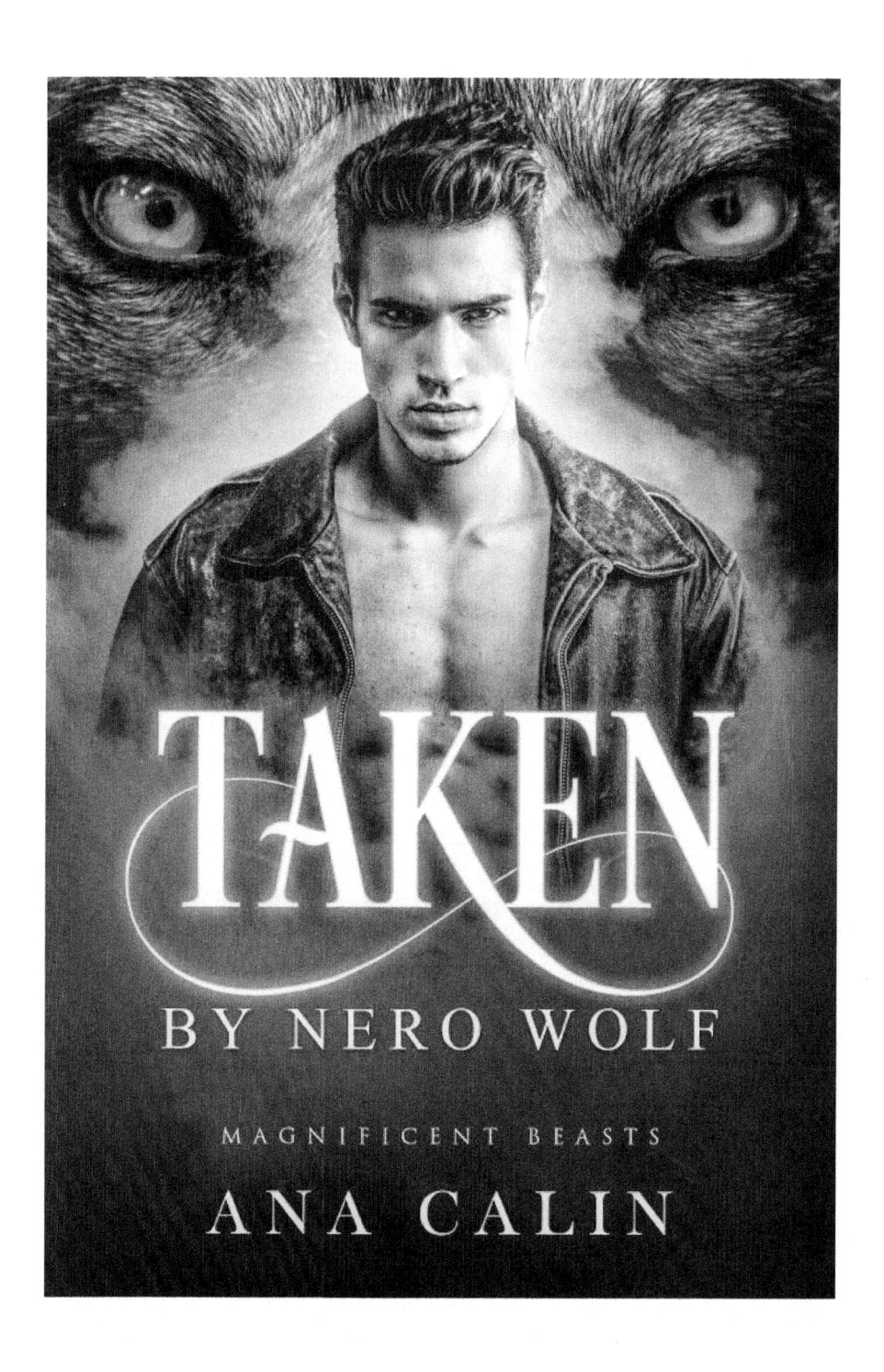

BY NERO WOLF

MAGNIFICENT BEASTS

ANA CALIN

ALL RIGHTS RESERVED
No part of this book may be reproduced or transmitted in
any form or by any means, electronic or mechanical,
including photocopying, recording, or by any information storage
and retrieval system, without permission in writing
from the author except in the case of brief quotations
embodied in reviews.
Publisher's Note:
This is a work of fiction,
the work of the author's imagination.
Any resemblance to real persons or events is
coincidental.

———

Copyright June 2019 – Ana Calin

Table of Contents

Title Page 1
Copyright Page 2
CHAPTER I 4
CHAPTER II 18
CHAPTER III 33
CHAPTER IV 44
CHAPTER V 57
CHAPTER VI 80
CHAPTER VII 97

CHAPTER I

Princess

I stand in the middle of the Council Room, clutching my resignation. The double doors open, and the sound of chairs pushing back pierces my ears. Six Council members stand up on each side of the hall, while I remain stiff by the large desk, watching the two bodyguards walk in first, opening the way for the new mayor.

This isn't the first time I've seen Nero Wolf, the powerful leader of the werewolf pack that took over our town, but it's the first time I've seen him in person. He doesn't have an online profile, but my bff, his brother's wife, showed me pictures.

"He's imposing to say the least," she said. "If you're not prepared, his looks might strike you dumb. I've seen it happen before."

And she was right. He is striking, with a crushing presence, you can feel it from the moment you see him.

Everybody watches him as he heads down the kingly hall to the desk with the huge window behind it that presides over Darkwood Falls. He stops on the side of the desk opposite from me.

Picture or no, I didn't expect Nero Wolf to be so tall, taller than everyone in the room, even taller than his brothers. He has the face of a ruthless young angel, the broad shoulders of a swimmer, and a very domineering air.

I can't hold his stare for long, my eyes falling to his carnal lips with their masculine shape. I refuse to find him attractive, but it's pure folly. The guy is handsome as fuck, standing here in his fitted black suit. I swallow the lump in my throat and hold out my resignation.

"I quit." I had a whole speech ready, but hell, I forgot it.

Nero Wolf's golden eyes fall down to the paper for only a moment. He heads to the mayor's chair, turns it around, and takes a seat like a king on his throne.

"Rejected."

"Excuse me? But I don't want this job, Mr. Mayor, and you *have to* respect my wish."

"Yes, I've heard that you're used to having your way, Miss Princess Skye. Your daddy got you this job, and Mr. Haan, the former mayor, was probably more in your service than you were in his, but in real life things work differently." He shows me to a chair by the door. "Now, if you don't mind, take your seat so we can start the first Council meeting. Make sure you write down the minutes."

Enraged, I slap my hands on the desk, leaning down to him. My face is burning so hot that I start to sweat.

"I'm well aware of how things really work in the world, and guess what—I'm going to learn more of it, because I intend to leave Darkwood Falls. I'm going out into the world, and I'll be operating by all its rules, thank you."

He studies me coolly for a moment.

"No one leaves Darkwood Falls, Miss Skye, not until we have shut down Sullivan Haan's threat completely. We all know he's lurking out there with his people, ready to prey on anyone from this town and use them to regain his place."

Of course, he doesn't mention the serpent shifters because no one in here knows what Sullivan truly is, as they have no idea that he, Nero Wolf, is half man half beast. They think Sullivan took off with the tax money, and would seek to support a dictatorial regime at the country's top so he can return as mayor to Darkwood Falls, this time with complete power.

"Now, if you don't mind, prepare to write down the minutes of the meeting," Nero concludes.

"Yes, Princess," Lord Theodore Fritz, member of the Council, puts in, his voice slimy for all its fake kindness. He used to be the sweetest tongue inside Sullivan's ear. He places soft hands on my shoulders. "Think about it, no one can help the new mayor better than you. Stay in his service, do it for the town's people."

I shrug him off, returning my angry attention to Nero, who now stares at me without blinking, making me feel his crushing power all the way to my bones.

"The only reason you want me here is because I'm a suspect, and I know that all too well, Mr. Mayor. But I assure you, I don't know any more about Sullivan Haan's business than I already told your brothers Drago and Conan, and you'd truly be better off with a new secretary. Someone for whom it'll be a pleasure to make you coffee and write down the minutes of your meetings. May I suggest Christie Yves, the barmaid. She's been looking for a way out of that slum of a pub for a lifetime, and I genuinely believe she's worth a chance."

Nero rises from his chair, swiping my letter of resignation from the desk. He walks slowly as he reads it, keeping his attention on the paper as he approaches me. I move instinctively out of his way to let him place himself in front of me, and lean on the desk.

I'll be damned. This close the man seems so big he blocks out the light.

"Miss Skye, if that's all right, I'd like to ask you a few questions. None of them are personal, and they're all related to City Hall and your work as a secretary. Will you answer them, truthfully, in front of the entire Council?"

"I will." Anything to get me off the hook and out of here. Nero Wolf's very presence is hard to bear.

"Is it true that the former mayor hired you at your father's insistences?"

"No, not insistences." I jut out my chin. "At his suggestion. He only needed make it once."

"Hmm." He tilts his head to the side, lowering my resignation letter and gripping the edge of his desk with both hands. His white shirt opens a little at his neck, revealing smooth bronze skin that contrasts beautifully with the white fabric. "But your father, Charles Skye, was also one of the former mayor's strongest supporters, and he also financed his campaigns, am I right?"

I press my lips together, sensing the Council's hawkish eyes on me. I feel Lord Theodore's strongest.

"Mr. Mayor, if all these questions are meant to expose me as some kind of parasite inside City Hall, someone who's done anything but earn her position here, then I'll admit to that." People gasp, and the gold in Nero's eyes glints at my words. Satisfaction fills me—I got you, handsome bastard; you didn't see this one coming. "I trust it also gives you more reason to let me go."

Without waiting for a response I turn on my heel, and start toward the doors. My head is hot with rage, the Council members swimming at the periphery of my vision. I place my hand on the doorknob, determined to leave this hall and never come back, but Nero Wolf's deep vibrant voice stops me before I can turn it.

"Your admission only provides me with more reason to keep you around, Miss Skye. Like I said, you are not to leave Darkwood Falls or renounce your service to City Hall until the serpents' threat is finally eliminated, and your connection to the former mayor cleared."

I whip around, looking daggers at him. "You can't do this, you can't *force* me to keep working for you."

"Consider it a necessary part of the investigation against Mr. Sullivan Haan." He pushes his big hands inside the pockets of his fitted slacks. "This is a matter of security, Miss Skye. I will keep you in the service of City Hall until the air has completely cleared, and that's the end of it."

There's nothing I want more than to keep defying him, but he turns around to re-take his seat at the mayor's desk, a clear sign the conversation is over. But there's still one thing I can do to defy him, and that is to leave the hall before he begins his first meeting with the Council. I won't write down the minutes even if he drags me back with his own hand.

"This isn't my last word on this, Mr. Mayor," I say before I leave, squaring my shoulders. If he wants war with me, that's what he'll get. Good luck keeping a grip on this wild girl, Nero Wolf, Alpha of your pack and new interim mayor of Darkwood Falls. I've been kept in chains for far too long, I won't be imprisoned again.

※

Nero

EVENING HAS COME, STARLIGHT flowing through the big window behind me as I read Sullivan's files on the laptop. It's peaceful, and I'm completely focused until one of the guards barges in with a wild look on his face, the doors thudding against the walls.

"Mr. Mayor, it's Miss Skye. She's at a bar downtown, getting wasted with tourist men. Things are getting out of hand." He flushes. "I'm sorry, but I think she's about to take one home. Or some place for, you know, sex."

"And why are you barging in here about it? Why didn't you stop her, that's why I had you follow her."

"I tried to intervene, Mr. Mayor, but—" He wrings his hands like he's afraid to say it, but he goes for it in the end. "She wouldn't be dissuaded no matter what I do. You said we weren't allowed to force her into anything physically, but I'm afraid that would be the only solution. The boys stayed back to make sure she at least doesn't leave the pub until I could come and get you, but I'm not sure they'll be able to keep her in there without using force. I tried to call on your cell, but it's off. Miss Skye didn't activate redirection of calls before she left, so I couldn't reach your office either."

I close the classified file, secure the laptop, and stalk towards the exit.

"Call your boys, and tell them to keep her there until I arrive, no matter what. As for you, you're dismissed for the night."

"Let me come with you, Sir. You can't go around Darkwood Falls without protection. There are people who didn't approve of the Council's electing you as interim mayor, it might be dangerous for you out there."

"Things are rarely dangerous for me, so relax." I stop at the door and turn to the concerned young man. "What's your name?"

"Cole, Sir. Jordan Cole."

"You've done a good job today, Jordan. Now go get some rest. Looks like you need it."

I walk out of City Hall and get inside the Porsche. Truth is, the last thing I expected on my first day as interim mayor of Darkwood Falls was having to deal with a frustrated little princess that will do anything for attention.

I decide to make a short stop at Arianna and Drago's place, since it's on my way. If anyone can give me a tip or two on how to deal with the girl, then it's Arianna, my new sister-in-law, and Princess's best friend. I can also use the chance to change, this suit is ridiculously fancy for the downtown pubs full of both locals and tourists that I'm going to.

The housekeeper opens the door, since Arianna is far too pregnant, and can barely still move around. I find her in the living room, having tea and reading a book.

"Sorry, I can't get up for a hug. I've come to need Drago's help for everything," she says after I give her a kiss on the cheek.

"It's hard with two werewolf babies in your belly, different from a purely human pregnancy," I explain quietly after I've thrown a glance over my shoulder, making sure the housekeeper has returned to the kitchen.

"Well, I'm glad that Drago agreed that we live here, in Darkwood Falls, in the end. I know how things work in this in town, and I trust the hospital. The chief of obstetrics is an old friend, and I'm pretty sure we can trust her with our secret, if we need to when the time comes."

I smile warmly down at her. "I can't wait to meet and hold my niece and nephew. They will be the most beautiful thing that has happened to me in centuries. Now, if you don't mind, I'll borrow some clothes from your husband. I need to go collect your friend Princess Skye from a pub where she apparently got drunk beat, and I don't think I can go like this."

"Princess, drunk beat? Why?"

"I rejected her resignation today, but she wouldn't have it. Now she got tipsy, and is aggressively picking up men, to make a point, I guess. The bodyguards I sent to keep an eye on her won't let her leave the pub with any of the guys, but I'm afraid they won't be able to do much if she insists, since I forbade them to lay a hand on her."

Concern shadows Arianna's face. "Drinking like that is out of character for Princess. I mean, while she likes to flirt, and she enjoys her cocktails, she doesn't normally get *drunk beat*. She must be seriously upset, which can only mean that you accused her again of leaking information to Sullivan. I told you before, and I'll tell you as often as I must, she's not the one."

"I know you trust her, Arianna, and maybe you're right in doing so, but I have to take protective measures until we're certain. She has been working for him longer than anyone else. It's very likely she knows more than she lets on."

Arianna wants to protest, but I've already started up the stairs. We see things differently in this case, Arianna and I, and I don't want to spoil a perfectly nice in-laws relationship.

"I better hurry and try to clarify things with her," I throw over my shoulder.

I take two stairs at a time, and enter Arianna and Drago's dressing room. I know Drago wanted to build her something bigger when they renovated the house, after he fought three serpents in her room and nearly demolished everything, but she decided she wanted to keep the house the way it was when her parents still lived here.

I open the neckline of my shirt, and slide Drago's leather jacket off the coat hanger. My legs are longer than Drago's, so I pick a pair of ripped jeans and army boots that go over my ankles so it looks like the jeans fit, then head back down the stairs.

"Please let me know when she's safe," Arianna calls after me before I close the door and slide behind the wheel of the Porsche. I charge my phone in the car and call one of the bodyguards.

"Whatever you do, don't let her go. I'll be right there."

"You better hurry, boss," comes the answer. *"She's got men around her like bears around a honey pot."*

Funny twist of fate that the pub where I find Princess is called The Big Bad Wolf. She stands out with her red hair that tumbles down her back in sleek curls. The woman clearly likes being the center of attention, and right now she's a fucking lighthouse.

Being the tallest guy in the over-crowded pub, I can see clearly what is going on down at the bar. At least five guys are gathered around Miss Princess Skye. No wonder they're all so taken with her. Even the way she holds her cocktail is seductive—I wonder how many she's already had. The guy she's talking to, a young man with spiked hair and a Casanova grin, is enjoying her undeterred attention at this moment.

I make my way closer, ignoring all the women checking me out like I'm candy as I watch Princess's lips move. She has a hypnotic effect on these men, and that can only mean she has experience in the art of seduction.

I heard she used to secretly get out of Darkwood Falls in Sullivan's day, and pick up men at bars in nearby towns. This is one of the reasons I suspect she had a special relationship with the former mayor—she made it out of Darkwood Falls a lot more often than any other high-born girl of this town, including Arianna.

Princess has experience in turning heads, that much is obvious. I can tell from the way she moves her body, and the way she bats those long black lashes that hood her mysterious eyes the color of caramel. Poor bastards don't stand a chance. I keep my eyes fixed on her as I approach, adjusting my route so that she doesn't see me incoming.

The guy closest to her back moves out of my way instinctively. Most men do when I have my eyes set on a prey like this. I may still be a man on the outside, but on the inside I'm already in wolf mode, and they sense it. I bend close to Princess, my breath touching her bare shoulder. She's taken off the white shirt she was wearing at City Hall, revealing her skin that is white and translucent, like a fairy's, contrasting in a very sexy way with her black corset. Her outfit is extravagant, but she wears it with a style that few women can pull off. Hell, even I like it, and I'm not easily impressed.

"I thought I'd made myself clear," I say low in her ear. "You're not to date strangers—yet. Not as long as anyone could be a serpent spy."

What I can see of her white, fine-muscled back tightens.

"I thought I'd made myself clear as well, Mr. Mayor," she retorts. Her chin juts out as she offers me her paper-white profile. "I will do as I please, no matter whether you approve or not." A pleasant scent wafts from her hair, and I can't help but bury my nose in a silky strand.

"Mate, can't you see that you're intruding?" the guy with the spiked hair says. My nostrils flare as my eyes shoot to him.

"Back off, boy," I grunt. "The girl is with me." Now why the fuck did I just say that?

"No, she's not," Princess says, both to me and the guy with the spikes. The guy's eyes fall to her lips, and I swear I could rip his fucking head off. "I didn't come here with him, and I'm not going to leave with him either."

Everything in Princess's attitude encourages the poor bastard to fight for her. He steps down from his barstool, determined to impress the girl, and completely oblivious to the fact that he's facing a beast that could literally tear him apart.

"Stand down, Spikes," I grunt a warning. I can sense all the other guys around take a step back, feeling the threat in their bones. I'm a burning beast on the inside, and they can fucking feel it, but the idiotic Spikes seems to have more at stake than all of them. I narrow my eyes as I wonder what reason he could possibly have to act against the cautioning of his own instincts, and dare to challenge me.

"You heard the lady, big guy. You can leave now, before you embarrass yourself."

I don't move, letting him approach and ready to teach him a hard lesson.

"I said," he presses, while the others watch tensely. "Get away from the lady."

He's now standing only inches away from me, but he's almost a head smaller. Focused on Princess I hadn't noticed the film of sweat on his face and the sickly pallor of his skin, but it jumps out at me now. The boy seems ill.

"Go away." He slaps the back of his hands against my chest. I don't move an inch, but he tries again. Only this time I catch his wrist in the air and twist it behind his back, forcing him down.

"Fuck me!" Spikes falls to one knee, throwing his head back, his face distorted in pain. "What the fuck man, let me go."

Under any other circumstances I would. I've already made an example out of him, and that's all I wanted, in case any of the others were thinking of taking a chance, too. But the tattoo on the inside of Spikes' now twisted wrist draws my attention.

"A serpent in the shape of a dollar sign," I say, just loud enough that Princess hears it as well. She's sitting rigid on her stool, her mouth open at what's she's just witnessed, her chest rising and falling fast as she breathes. She's scared, anxious and, judging by her scent, also horny.

I yank the boy up and haul him around, slamming him against the bar. Glasses fly, the bartender pushes back against the shelves, and people start screaming behind me. Must be because I lifted a heavy looking guy from the ground as if he weighed nothing, and now I'm handling him like he's a doll. My hands firm on Spikes' lapels, I glance over my shoulder to my men by the exit.

"Seal the door. Nobody gets in or out. Serpents' scouts."

They bolt the door, radioing their colleagues, and keeping those trying to trickle away inside. My men are human, but well-trained and armed.

"What the hell is going on?" Princess says in the high-pitched voice that only fear can cause.

I slam Spikes against the bar, really hard this time, making him grunt as his bones crack.

"Christ's sakes, what are doing to him?" Princess shrieks.

"He and maybe all the other guys around you are serpents' men," I hiss between my teeth, my eyes blazing golden at her. Blood boils beneath my skin, and I'm dangerously close to shifting. I can feel my skin thickening, fur pushing to sprout right beneath it. "Have you been confederating with them? Did you get them to meet you here?"

"What the hell are you talking about, no!" She jumps off the bar stool, grabs her designer bag with a furious look on her face, and stomps to the door. The boys stop her from getting out, while I return my attention to Spikes.

"Tell me who sent you boy, and why, or I swear to God I'll tear your head from your shoulders."

He stares horrified at my growing fangs, my upper lip already curling like a snout.

"Talk." I'm already thinking of taking him outside in the back alley and cornering him by the dumpsters. People of Darkwood Falls don't know about werewolves and serpents, at least not all of them and not officially, so I can't shift in here where everyone can see.

"What do you mean you're not letting me go," Princess demands by the door. "Move out of the way at once, or—"

But before she can finish, Spikes starts to choke in my hands, his eyes rolling back, foam trickling out from the corners of his mouth. I take my hands off of him, letting him drop to the floor, lest people think it's me who's doing this to him. But he begins twisting like a man possessed, his neck swelling as if something's strangling him from the inside.

A few moments later he stills on the floor, only his limbs twitching. Then I see it, the small head of a viper, slithering its way out of his mouth. I squash it under my boot before anyone else can see. Fuck, the serpents put voodoo snakes inside their acolytes to make sure they died before they could betray their masters.

I turn around to see Princess standing shocked by the door, her big caramel eyes fixed on the dead guy. I open my mouth to command the men to check everyone's wrists for the serpents' mark, but Princess begins trembling, and I panic—is there one inside her, too? No, it can't be, this can't be happening to her!

I stride over so fast that the air whirls around me, not even trying to mask my superhuman speed. All that matters is helping Princess in any way I can. I get there right before she bends from her waist, crouching down and bracing her knees as if she's sick. I hunker down with her, my heart pounding—I cannot lose her, she's far too important; important to the werewolves' mission in Darkwood Falls, important in taking down the serpents, important in so many ways.

The perfume that filters into my nostrils from her hair strengthens the sensation that this woman matters more than anything else. I pull out my phone from my pocket, placing the other hand on Princess's back, her skin like velvet against my rough palm. My brother picks up after the first ring.

"Drago, I need you here ASAP."

༺✦༻

Princess

I'M INSIDE NERO WOLF'S convertible Porsche, riding into the night, the summer breeze blowing my hair.

"Where are you taking me," I manage.

"Home," comes Nero's deep, vibrant voice. It's pleasant, like a ripple of chocolate.

"No, not home, please. My dad is there, he can't see me like this. And he can't see me with you."

"You have a big house, Miss Skye, almost a palace. He won't see us. Besides, I'll bring you inside, then I'll leave."

"But what if I'm not safe there, Nero?" I can feel his eyes pierce the darkness as they snap to me.

"So we're on first name terms now?"

"On whatever terms will make you understand."

"I'll gladly listen to whatever you have to tell me, Princess. What do you think threatens your safety?"

I watch him driving, his wolfish eyes fixed ahead, his leather jacket tight on his long, muscular arms. He's handsome as fuck, damn it.

"Why don't you feel safe at your place, Princess?" he insists softly, his voice still deep, but no longer commanding. It's pleasant, accommodating as if I could tell him anything, almost like a shrink's.

"Listen Nero, I'm not keeping things from you, like you think I am, I wasn't in on Sullivan's shady business." I bite my lip, thinking of ways to tell him this. He keeps watching the road in the headlights, the summer breeze bringing the scent of the woods. "But I'm afraid my father was."

I wait to see how he reacts to that. But not a muscle moves on his face.

"Yes," he encourages softly. Seems he already knew, or at least expected it.

"It's no secret to you that my dad used to finance Sullivan's campaigns. I always wondered why. He never even liked Sullivan, on the contrary. But I always had the feeling Sullivan had something on him, on my dad, you know. Something dirty enough to force him to finance his campaigns and more than that. Dad kept much of his business with him secret, and ever since Sullivan disappeared, even more so. He seals doors and windows, paranoid someone might get into the house and kill him." I bite my lip. I can't really focus on what I have to say anymore. These sensations inside, the burning in my core is growing worse. I fan myself with my hand, hot and thinking about sex, which I'm afraid shows in my every move and even in my voice.

"If the serpents wanted your father dead, they would have killed him by now. But I'll have people guard your house starting tonight." He glances at me. "But our main problem is that it seems the serpents are targeting *you*. I'll stay with you tonight, make sure you're safe. I'll check the entire perimeter and won't leave until everything is secured."

My heart jumps. "Yes, I'd be grateful for that." Fuck, he's going to spend the night with me. "What do you think that guy with the tattoo wanted from me?"

"I don't know for sure, but I know he put something in your drink, and we need to find out what. It could be poison, for all we know."

He presses those carnal lips together, and a flash shoots up from my core to my chest. Damn it, I want those lips on mine, I want to know what they feel like.

"I'm not feeling very well, to be honest. I can't get this heat out of my body." I touch my neck with both hands, moving them down to my chest.

"What are you doing?"

The heat is unbearable, right beneath my skin. All I know is that I need his big rough hands doing what my own are doing. "I always liked your voice, ever since I heard you on the phone."

He doesn't reply, his eyes moving from the road to me and back again, as if he's trying to diagnose me as he drives.

"I mean it, Nero." I squirm in the leather seat, pressing my thighs together and arching from my waist. *What the fuck are you doing* screams in my head, but I'm losing my mind by the second as if I'm drunk, Nero's scent of wild forest working on me like an aphrodisiac. I close my eyes and sniff the air, tracing his scent on it.

"Damn, you smell as wild as you look. You smell of the jungle." Fuck, my rational brain must have completely shut off.

Nero takes a turn into a side dirt road and pulls over. The headlights illuminate fir trees that seem taken out of a fairy tale, the falls rushing in the distance. I'm worried that he'll laugh at me, that I'm making a complete fool out of myself, but fuck, I'm horny. I need his big rough hands on my hips, his big Alpha werewolf cock plunging inside of me from behind, at the cost of him seeing me as a cheap wanton for the rest of my life. The price is high, what's left of my rational mind screams at me that it is, but this excitement is more powerful than anything else.

"Oh, Nero, you big bad wolf. To be completely honest, all I can think about right now is you bending me over the hood of your big black car."

"That's not going to happen," he says, his voice deep. He's not pissed, but not impressed either. Sure, hundreds of women must have hit on him before me, it's not like I'm anything special. He is a magnificent beast, the kind of man who could be every girl's type. Heat courses through my body in waves, stripping away all my defenses and self-imposed limitations—he is Nero Wolf, the Alpha of the werewolf pack that's taken over the town, an unbearably handsome beast that doesn't trust me in the least.

"I'd never take advantage of you," he says.

"Not even if I beg you to?"

This need in my core grows more intense by the minute, and my heart is now beating like a rabbit's. Excitement turns to fear—what the hell is happening to me, why do I feel like I'll die if I don't feel Nero Wolf's big hard cock inside of me?

"I think Spikes put a sex drug in your drink," Nero says as my hand trickles down between my legs, under my red mini skirt. "Princess, please stop that."

I stare at the chiseled edges of his face, his intense eyes and those masculine, carnal lips. Damn, how I want those hot lips on mine.

"I think it's some kind of substance that makes you crave sex like crazy," he says, keeping his cool. I feel stupid, since it doesn't seem I have any effect on him. Sure, what did I expect. He's the hottest guy I've ever met, a beast of a man, women must offer themselves to him on golden platters. But I can't control the way my body reacts to him, no matter how much I will myself to.

I moan as I slip my finger under my panties and stroke my shaved folds. God, my senses are heightened.

"Forgive me," I slur, mortified to the core yet unable to stop. "But it feels like I'm going to die if I don't find release." My body twists in the leather seat as I search for my own orgasm.

Nero's eyes flash golden. He seems a wild beast, which should give me the creeps, but all I can think about is sex with him.

He bends down to me, his golden eyes alight, and my heart leaps into my throat. I'm sure he's going to kiss me, certain that I'll finally feel those carnal masculine lips on mine, but no. He takes my chin between two rough fingers, and inspects me in the light of his wolfish eyes that seem to work as flashlights, illuminating my face.

"Relax, Princess. You're perfectly safe with me, and nothing can happen to change that. I won't take advantage of your substance-induced excitability, but I'll make sure you'll be fine." His voice, deep and pleasant like melted chocolate, makes me relax, a feeling of trust engulfing me. Is this the magical power Arianna was telling me about? Werewolves being able to influence people's moods, making them feel more relaxed, to the point of anesthetizing them even in the face of the most shocking things?

But despite the relaxation the substance keeps working in my body. The more I give in to Nero's pleasant control over my mood, the more the heat ravages my veins and my skin like some cursed poison, and I panic. A look deep into Nero's eyes confirms my terrifying hunch—whatever that serpents' minion put inside my body, it's going to kill me.

CHAPTER II

Nero

I take her pretty face between my hands. Her cheeks are small and hot against my palms as big as a bear's paws, her silky red hair flowing between my fingers. The sensation is exquisite, and it goes to my head like an aphrodisiac. This has never happened before, not in over five hundred years, and it can spell big trouble. But something else is at stake, something much bigger than my feelings—this woman might die in my arms tonight.

"Princess, I can use my senses to trace the poison in your blood, but it would take time we don't have. I need you to listen to me carefully. Usually people in desperate situations can sense what it is they need in order to survive. The body is as intelligent as the whole universe. I can prove that to you, and I promise I will some day, but right now I need you to take my word for it."

I keep my powers activated on her, sending the chemicals of calm coursing through her veins, while also prompting her to listen to the rest of her chemistry that tells her what to do.

Her heavy dark lashes flutter over her pretty caramel eyes that now seem fluid with desire. She raises her hand and touches my jaw, her lips parting as if touching me is pure delight.

"I need you to kiss me, Nero," she whispers, her breath close to my face.

Want pools in my groin. Fuck, we're so close to each other, only a few inches of air between us, air that feels burning hot.

"I can't do that, Princess, no matter what."

"But I'm dying, Nero. Whatever thing that bastard put in my drink, it's ravaging me on the inside, and it will keep doing it if I don't...."

If she doesn't cum. She doesn't need to finish the sentence, I understand it from her body chemistry that I'm probing deeper. I trace the poison and it is, indeed, deadly, unless an orgasm changes her chemistry, fast.

"I won't take advantage of you." Though my body is screaming to take her like I own her.

"You'd be saving me."

I never had to fight my body like this in my life. Her scent, her silky hair between my fingers, her slightly parted plump lips, all of it is doing scary shit to me. Must be because of her altered body chemistry that's playing wild because of the poison, making her feel and smell like a... It hits me—Princess Skye is a fated female, and the poison has unlocked her chemistry.

I don't dare move, afraid that even sniffing her arousal will have me shift into a beast roaring to have her, but Princess is on fire. She lifts her chin, her lips now brushing mine.

"Please, Nero," she whispers, her breath hot on my mouth. "You'd be saving my life."

"Oh, Princess." I lose the battle with myself, my mouth claiming those forbidden cherry red lips. They taste sweet as sin, as the apple of Eden must have tasted to Adam, a taste so unique that I lose myself in it.

Waves of heat run through me, molten desire ripples under my skin.

I lose it. I trap Princess between my body and the car seat, keeping my mouth locked on hers, but throwing off my leather jacket and ripping the shirt off my body. I break the kiss, my eyes burning as I stare into hers. She stares back awe-struck, red-cheeked and wide eyed as if she can't believe what's happening.

I trace her jaw with my thumb as I talk, doing nothing to hide my lust.

"I may shift into a werewolf while I do this. No matter what you think you know about us, it'll be shocking, and it will be scary."

"I don't care," she says, raising her face for a kiss, pressing those hot plump lips to mine.

"Princess," I manage, putting a finger between our mouths. "You should care because I will shift, it's a fact. Are you sure you want to—" Fuck, it sounds bad. "You want to sleep with a beast?"

"I want you to take me like it's your birth right, Nero." She pushes my hand aside and kisses me again, her tongue stroking my lips, her flesh releasing the maddening scent that can only be a fated female's.

I kiss her neck and her chest like a mad man, ripping the black corset off of her. Tits as round and firm as apples spring free, her nipples pink and perky. I growl, my skin hardening, fur pushing to sprout out from under it.

I lick and kiss Princess's tits in a fever, shifting at the same time. On the outside this must look like a scene from some kind of erotic horror movie—A half-naked beauty in a car, being ravished by a huge beast, his tongue on her tits, and his paws all over her. But I keep my hands in the half-state between human and beast, thick strong fingers finding their way into her panties.

"Fuck, your folds feel soft as cream," I growl, my brain on fire. Princess pushes her tits out, pressing both of her hands on mine between her legs. She pushes my fingers inside of her, eyes fixed on my face while I go deeper into the tight hotness of her pussy.

I swear this must be the most ravishing scene I've seen in my life. This woman naked in my car, her skin white as alabaster, red waves of silky hair tumbling down around her slim round shoulders. I touch her cheek with my other hand, my beast finger thick and rough against her delicate skin.

"You're a vision," I whisper, but the sound comes out deep and gruff from my chest. Princess takes my hand in hers, her eyes like dreamy and full of desire.

"I want you to fuck my mouth, Nero, in your beast form."

I swallow, struggling to control the turmoil inside.

"This is the poison speaking. You need an orgasm, and you need it fast."

"I'm going to cum while I suck your cock, and then I'm going to cum again when you take me on the hood of your car."

Fuck, the movie she puts in my head. I growl, pushing her seat back and easing my hand out of her pussy, rising to my feet. Without a second thought I grab her red hair with one hand, and undo my belt and jeans with the other. The clothes would have been torn to pieces if I'd fully shifted, but right now I'm half man half beast, my cock big and ribbed as I push it inside Princess's plump mouth.

Jesus Christ, the sensation....

I scent the chemicals running wild inside her body as she sucks with zeal, milking the pleasure out of my cock. She looks up at me as she moves back and forth along my length, showing her pleasure at playing a wanton, sucking off a beast. It turns her on wildly, I can scent it in her body chemistry.

"Stop." I want to retreat, because I'm too close to cumming, but Princess grabs my ass, demanding I stay. I growl as my sperm squirts out, and only then Princess lets go of my cock, pushing her tits up and watching with wicked satisfaction as I cum on them, my sperm dripping off her nipples.

I breathe hard, staring down at her, my head swimming. How is it possible for this woman to make me feel things no other woman ever came even close to, and how can I want her even more now that I've had her.

"Now bend me over the hood of your car and bang me like you own me."

Sweet Jesus, the delight on her heated face while she says that, the lava in her eyes. Impulses fire inside of me, making me feel so alive that my life before this seems to have been a waste, as if I was only half alive. I scoop her up and jump with her onto the thick grass, placing her on her feet in the headlights in front of the car.

I rip her mini skirt, her stockings and her panties off of her, and drink in the sight of her. She's standing naked in front of me, her tits covered in my cum, her red hair messed up, and her mouth swollen from sucking my cock.

"I'm going to fuck you now," I decree in my deep beast voice. "But I won't bend you over the hood. I'll look you in the face while I drive my cock inside of you."

※

Princess

THE ALPHA OF THE WEREWOLF pack closes his rough hands on my hips, hoisting me onto the hood of his black Porsche. Now that he's had his release he's turned fully back into a human, into the heartbreakingly handsome Nero Wolf.

My eyes lick down his athletic body, my hands splaying over his chest. Feeling his rock-hard muscles under my palms makes me so fucking horny I'm soaking wet.

"I want you to fuck me hard," I demand, drunk with desire as I'm staring into the werewolf's golden eyes.

I open my legs to let him position himself between them. He's unusually tall, so he has to plant his legs apart and bend his knees so he can push that big ribbed cock inside of me. I mewl as he fills me, forcing my walls apart.

"You like having a big thick cock fill you, don't you, Princess." His voice is a dangerous dark ripple, the sharp features of his face making me feel at the mercy of a bad boy.

"Fuck, you need a special permit for that weapon of a cock." I whine as he pulls back only to push inside of me again, this time deeper, giving me both pleasure and pain. Soon he fucks me like there's no tomorrow, one hand fisted in my hair, and tugging my head back, the other one pushing a finger inside my butt. Sweet Jesus, the sensation is out of this world.

"Forgive me," he says gruffly. "But it'll speed things up, and we have to neutralize that poison fast."

"Oh, God, yes," I scream, pleasure exploding from deep inside me, coating Nero's werewolf cock in my female cum. The way he tugged my hair and fucked my ass with his finger while driving his iron-hard rod into my pussy was a head-spinning experience that leaves me sprawled on the hood of his car, spent and dizzy.

Minutes later the pleasure still hasn't completely subsided, but my mind is clearing. The more I realize what just happened, the more shame takes over me. I prop myself on my hands and make to bring myself to a sitting position, but Nero is quick to help me up.

Jesus. I look right up into his golden eyes, slowly down his strong features to his broad chest and finally down to the place where we're still connected between my legs.

"Oh my God this is so embarrassing," I manage in a trembling voice as Nero eases himself out of me. I'm sure he must think I'm the dirtiest wanton woman that ever existed, having offered myself to him like this, in the woods, asking to be taken in these shameful ways.

But instead of zipping up and inviting me into the car coolly, as I expected he would, he cups his hard-on with his large hand and begins stroking, and I realize he hasn't cum yet.

"Don't worry," he breathes, as if he knows what I'm thinking. "You don't have to do anything, but let me look at you while I finish off."

Pleasure runs through my body at those words. I still have a little while left with him. I slide off the hood, and he lets me do it, but when I drop to my knees and grab his cock to stick it into my mouth, he stops me.

"No, you don't have to do this."

"You let me do it before." I look up his magnificent muscular body into his face, and my pussy throbs for him again. How can I want him so badly after only a few minutes since a shattering orgasm?

"You were in danger of dying, Princess, otherwise I wouldn't have dared to. The climax changed your body chemistry, and reversed the effect of the substance. You're yourself again now, you don't have to give pleasure to a man you don't truly want."

"Oh, but I do want you, Nero." The truth overfills my heart, and I can't keep it to myself. "I want you in ways I didn't even think it was possible to want a man."

Nero stills, puzzled, because he thought I hated his guts. I let the expression in my eyes change as I look up at him, now full of dirty desire. He doesn't try to stop me again when I close my lips around the wide crest of his iron cock, my jaw hurting from before. But I ignore the pain and take in as much of him as I can, though he's too big for me to take all of him.

To my surprise it takes only a few seconds of me moving back and forth along his length for Nero to growl like an animal, grab my hair and release his cum into my mouth. He tugs my hair to move me away at the last second, but I don't let him. I grab his muscular butt and keep him in my mouth, swallowing the hot salty waves of his masculine juice.

How will he ever believe that he's the first man whose sperm I swallow? The idea was enough to disgust me in the past, but with Nero, I want to take in every last drop of his sap, as if that is the essence of his commanding masculinity. I look up at him, a sculpted god, as he pumps my mouth until he's spent.

I let him out and lick my lips as his golden eyes land on me. He drops down to his knees, pulling me to his large, muscular chest, pressing my cheek to his hot skin. The moment I touch my face to the hair on his chest, the strangest sensation explodes inside of me, spreading from my core to the rest of my body—I feel home. If time were to stop and eternity were, indeed, a continuous now, then this right here is what I want to feel. Forever.

<hr>

Nero

DAMN. I JUST FUCKED my secretary.

Out of all the thoughts I could have right now, this is the first one that comes to mind.

"We should, err." I look down at this beautiful woman on her knees in front of me, completely naked and full of my cum. It's like I've claimed every inch of her body, marking her breasts with my essence as if to mark my territory. She looks back at me with hope in her caramel eyes, the hope to read in my face what she means to me now, after what happened between us.

I may not be the Casanova my brother Drago used to be, or the ladies' man Achilles still is, but I've had many women in my five centuries of life. I know what this look means, I can read the uncertainty as well as the desire for emotional connection in them. Princess is different from all of the women I had before, but what is it that I feel for her? What is this energy that seems to connect every inch of our bodies? Could it be that I—Fuck. Have I imprinted on her?

I jump up to my feet, trying to figure out what to do. My heart hammers in my chest like it's out of control, and I look everywhere around except at Princess Skye, the beautiful and fiery redhead I just made mine.

"Er, let's get you cleaned up." I get a larger piece of my torn shirt from the car and walk back to her.

I'm a fucking idiot. Now on her feet in front of me, Princess braces herself, covering her breasts and trembling. She keeps her eyes cast down, silky red waves of hair falling to shield her cheeks from my scrutiny. Even her feet point inward, another clear sign she feels mighty uncomfortable.

My heart breaks inside my chest as I begin wiping my juice off of her, realizing she must wish she were anywhere other than facing me right now, and that's all my fault. I urge myself to say something that will make her feel more comfortable, but it seems I've gone dumb. Nothing comes to mind, except,

"We'll be at your place soon, you'll be able to take a hot bath and relax."

She nods her head, but doesn't raise her eyes, and I suspect she might be crying. By the time I return from the trunk with a coat I keep for emergencies, intending to wrap her in it until we reach her house, Princess is sniffling.

I wrap the coat around her tightly, then I put on my own leather jacket, all the while thinking of things I could say to make this better. But what could I possibly say? Even if I considered having, I don't know, more with her than what happened tonight, how do I do it? I've never been in a relationship before, just a few longer sexual arrangements with women who professed they didn't want more, but ended up crying like Princess now. But, unlike her, they also argued vehemently I owed them a commitment. Even though they'd propositioned the no-strings-attached arrangement themselves, they argued I should have fallen in love, that that was the whole point of intimacy. They were probably right, but not even I could force my wolf to imprint on a woman who wasn't born for it.

On a woman who wasn't Princess Skye. The more I feel her by my side, the stronger the connection. For a moment I can even sense the sore feeling my cock has left inside of her.

I turn the Porsche into the road and drive to Princess' house. The wind blows through her wavy red hair, the sweet scent of her flesh reaching me in the breeze. My eyelids feel heavy, my nostrils flaring to take as much of it as I can.

"Can you stop here?" Princess says when we're near her place, her voice small. She pushes her hair behind her ear, revealing a side of her face for the first time since we left the woods, but she doesn't look at me. "If we pull into the driveway my dad could see from upstairs."

"All right, we'll take the back door."

We leave the car close to the woods behind Princess's impressive family manor. Though I help her by keeping a firm arm around her shoulders, Princess fails to keep her balance as we make our way through the thick layer of grass, small dunes and holes twisting her ankles. She barely makes a sound each time she stumbles or a twig scratches her legs, but I can't take her discomfort. My heart twists each time she experiences pain.

I scoop her up, tearing a yelp of surprise from her throat.

"I'll carry you."

With my face now so close to her again, her scent drives me crazy. A new need balls in my stomach, the need to pull her so close that her body becomes one with mine, to feel the velvety texture of her skin. I try to keep it inconspicuous when I bring my nose to the top of her head, inhaling the sweet perfume of her hair. She makes herself small at my chest, but I have this nagging feeling she's not doing it for the same reasons I am, namely for the need to feel me close, but rather to protect herself from my attention.

We approach the manor from the back yard. I always knew the place was impressive, but now that I'm so close to it I realize it seems a fortress. A few glances around is all I need to assess the perimeter before I call Conan and ask for a team to guard the Skye manor.

"I need a dozen well rested men," I tell him. "The way I see it, we'll have to infiltrate a few inside the house, too. It's big, labyrinthic, and the threat could come from everywhere, even from underneath."

I'm still in military assessment mode as Princess and I enter the big drawing room through the back terrace doors. The space is high and wide, resembling a ballroom more than it does a drawing room, even though there are couches with silken cushions, a big chimney and a big and tall bookcase that gives the room the elegant feel of an aristocratic library.

"Are there secret tunnels or passageways inside this house?" I inquire as my eyes dart around, calculating how every object could be used as a weapon, a shield or an advantage for the forces of evil.

"There are," Princess replies, walking to the bookcase and extracting something that looks like a parchment roll. It turns out it's drawings. "Here are the plans."

She walks to the fireplace, where I first think she wants to warm herself, but she pulls a lever and the fire dies, the wall behind it opening to a tunnel.

"We're gonna take one now to my room, lest my dad hears us about the house." She turns to me before she walks into the fireplace. "I think you need to see some of these passageways before you can instruct your men. Plus that I would very much appreciate it if you personally made sure the house, starting with my room, is secure before you leave."

With one look at the big portrait above the fireplace—Princess' megalomaniac father, I suppose—I step inside the fireplace, and the wall rises back into place behind us, connecting with an echoing thud back to the top of the fireplace.

"What happened to your mom?" I inquire as I follow her inside the tunnel. Unlike in creepy castles, this passageway is warm, cozy and nicely-lit with bulbs in the shape of oil lamps along the narrow walls.

"In New York for the summer fashion craze."

I watch her long red locks bounce as she leads the way. Fuck, how I want to grab those small shoulders and push her against the wall, parting her legs and taking her right here. It's the craving of my wolf—he wants to possess her inside this house so that he can make his claim on a core aspect of her life. A woman's parental home occupies a vital spot in her emotional body, and my Alpha wolf craves to possess that.

"You sound sad about it." I manage to sound cool, keeping my feelings from my voice.

"I'm not sad. It's just that she's never there, always has some society event to attend. She would drag me along, but since I haven't been allowed to leave Darkwood Falls until now, well. But, to be honest, it's mostly fashion shows, and even though I like them, I can't watch as many as Mom."

I want to ask her how come she doesn't model herself, her body is perfect for the catwalk—probably groomed into that by her mother—and her face is exquisite. She's extravagant and bold, the dream trophy wife for many a rich bastard. A lump forms in my throat and my jaw tightens at that thought. I fucking hate imagining that, and my wolf sends rage to my limbs. I remember how that now dead serpent servant leered at her, and a strange satisfaction about his death takes over.

Now there's something I should probably be worried about, but before I get to dwell on it Princess emerges into a hallway with a red rug running along its entire length. It leads down to a set of high double doors that she opens to enter what I suspect is her bedroom.

"Please close the doors behind you," she says over her shoulder, already throwing my coat off her shoulders.

Instead of closing the doors with my hands I push them shut by leaning with my back to them. I watch Princess walk naked toward the bathroom, and my cock starts to rise.

I bite my lips as those white hips sway, her buttocks round and firm, her hair falling like a wild red river down her back to her ass. The woman's body is a work of art with those long, dancer legs and finely-muscled arms. Her beauty is as extravagant as the outfits she wears; they do indeed represent her personality, which is also why she wears them with such style.

She stops in the doorway that leads to the bathroom.

"I'm going to take a bath."

"Yes, of course."

I'm devouring her with my eyes, and I'm aware of it, but I just can't stop myself. Her cheeks flush red and she disappears inside the bathroom.

I hear her turn the water on as I inspect the room where this exquisite female grew up. She spent most nights of her life here—except for the nights when she wasn't out having one night stands with bikers in neighboring towns. The idea pierces my heart like a swift blade, and I swear I can feel the blood gush out of it.

How many men has she had before me? Since I can't offer her a relationship, will she keep doing it, meet men and climax while riding them? I can see her riding some tattooed, hairy biker, her hips rocking as she climaxes for him; then I see him bend her over the leather seat of his Harley and the thought of murder clouds my head.

I'm driving myself crazy while I inspect the big queenly room with all its dark shades of red, the bed with the canopy up a dais, as well as her wardrobe. My face is burning, and my teeth crunching as porn movies of her and other guys play in my head.

"Is everything clear?" she says. I whip around to see her standing with a towel around her at the bathroom door, while I'm looking down at her from the dais by her bed.

"You can't leave Darkwood Falls again, and you can't even talk to strange men," I growl, low and menacing. Princess's perfectly drawn chocolate eyebrows rise as if she doesn't understand, but I don't care. I'll keep her in by force if I have to, I can't fucking live with the thought of her and some other guy.

"Do I make myself clear?" I demand.

Princess

HE STANDS THERE LIKE a king, telling me what I can and cannot do.

"Really, Nero? That's what's on your mind right now? I'd be more worried about the fact that serpents sent spies to this town to do crazy shit to people. Hell, maybe they're even after the Council."

"Which is exactly why I asked you—and all the other high-born women of Darkwood Falls—not to start dating or even flirting with outsiders just yet. Because I saw this coming." His eyes are blazing at me. I wish I could defy him, but I know he's right. I deserve the 'I told you so' that's written all over his face. I bite my lip, tighten the towel around me and cast my eyes down.

"I'm sorry about the way I came on to you tonight, by the way. It was shameless, I know, but I wasn't myself." Damn, this is awkward. I'm overwhelmed with emotion, a fact I'm trying to hide at the same time, which is exhausting. I feel shame, and anger, and hope and anger again. What the hell am I hoping for? Isn't it clear enough that Nero Wolf has remained cold as ice to me? That I'm nothing more than a one-night stand, one he didn't even want? He wouldn't have never slept with me under different circumstances.

"No, you weren't yourself. But none of this would have happened if you'd listened to me in the first place."

My head snaps up to him. His golden eyes narrow when he sees the red hotness in my cheeks and the frustration in my gaze.

"It's so easy for you to tell people what they should do or stop doing, isn't it? Tell them to stay put until their turn comes to be subjected to your scrutiny, and then scoff when they're restless about it. You made it clear from the start you suspected that I leaked to Sullivan, that I knew more about his dealings with the serpents than I was telling you guys. I was frustrated, angry, feeling powerless."

"That's true. What happened tonight is proof that you're, well, clean."

"Eureka." I would open my arms to make a point, but the towel would fall off of me. "Well, I should probably go change, restore some of my dignity by putting clothes on."

"You want to see me repent for having mistrusted you."

"I want to see you crawling at my feet, not just repent."

"You go change, Princess. I'll use the time to assess the surroundings, make sure everything's clear until my men have taken their position to protect the manor."

"Wait, you can't roam about the house, at least not before you've studied those plans I gave you. I don't want you running into my father."

"First of all, I would sniff out your father a mile away, like, right now, I know where he is in this house. I recognize his scent because it's got something of yours, and it's easy for me to trace. And secondly, I'll use my werewolf sharpened senses to inspect the surroundings, without even leaving this room. But I need to focus really hard to comb an area as wide as possible, and that means that I'll do something that looks like meditation. If I'm still at it when you come back, don't talk to me. It shouldn't take long, and I'll be back with you."

I nod and start toward the chamber adjacent to mine, a small room that I use as a dressing space. Picking a nightgown takes almost as long as picking a cocktail dress, because hell, the insanely sexy Nero Wolf is right next door in my room, and I want to be appealing to him. It's one of the ways I'll punish him, not only for his mistrust, but also for his coolness after we made love. Because that's what it was to me. Love-making, and it was beyond my wildest dreams, I never even imagined intimacy with a man could feel this good.

I want Nero to crave me, at least half as badly as I crave him. At least I can make him drool a little. I don't know if it's gonna make me feel any better, but at least I'll be doing something about this storm of emotions inside of me, this draining sense of need.

When I return to the bedroom I'm wearing a long silk nightgown—I chose a long one because I can't be obvious in what I'm trying to do. It's one of my favorite ones because the fabric is special quality, and stays true to the shape of my body. It feels like a river of silk flowing on my skin, making me look like a nymph.

Nero is standing at the window with his back at me, the leather jacket stretching on his broad shoulders. I stop by the bed and watch him, a god standing still in front of the big arched window, the velvet curtains aside. He seems to peer out into the night.

God, the man is beautiful. So beautiful in fact, that it's all too clear he's more than just a man. He's a magnificent beast, unusually tall and broad-shouldered. When he shifts, he turns into a huge wolf with fur so black he seems a devil with shiny golden eyes.

I wonder if he can feel my eyes slip down his frame as he stands there, peering out into the darkness, using his werewolf senses. Surely, like Drago, he can see the thick forests, the mountains, even the movement in them thanks to his superhuman werewolf abilities.

Now what do I do? Right, he said that he'd come to me when he's done scrutinizing the territory. I better make sure he finds me in a position that would make him want me again, or at least in a situation where he'll find me attractive. That's the only way for me to save a little bit of face after the shameless way I came on to him and had him take me.

I lay down on the soft bed, cringing every time it squeaks—it's an original vintage canopy bed, and creaks and squeaks come with the territory. But Nero doesn't move an inch. I lie down, hitching up the lower part of the gown in such a way that it falls sexy on my thigh. I put one knee up, lying on the big soft pillows with my hair spread around me.

And I wait.

And wait. For minutes, but apparently Nero needs time. I'm a bit worried that means he's found something, that Dad and I are truly in danger. But then I close my eyes and let his energy float to me, mingling with mine, and I feel safe. Safer than I've ever felt.

His energy does me good. My lids fall heavy, I let go of control, and tiredness fills me. It's been a long hard day. Started out with me defying the new mayor, enraged at his refusal to accept my resignation, then all the drinking at the pub, then the entire chaos that happened when Nero discovered the pub was full of serpents' acolytes and then... Jesus, then me shamelessly hitting on my boss on the first day I met him. That's not counting all the times I heard his deep, slow voice on the phone while he tried to get some truth out of me that he wanted to hear. I thought I'd hate him back then. Turns out that damn love hormone, oxytocin, is filling my veins now like crazy. I may be falling in love with him, fast and irrationally.

A thought soothes me—Tonight, even if only for a little while, we were lovers. I may not be anything special to Nero, too many women have wanted him in his life, maybe no woman can impress.

Except the one he will imprint on one day. I have no control over that, so I might just let go, try to keep the memory of what happened alive for as long as possible. Unlike werewolves' memory, humans' fade tragically quickly.

CHAPTER III

Nero

The perimeter is finally clear. My men are in place, and Drago is overseeing security tonight. I pull out my cell to call him and set up the meeting with the pack for tomorrow, turning around just the moment he picks up.

"Yes, Nero," he says, but I can't talk, staring with an open mouth at the scene in front of me. The beautiful Princess Skype lies asleep in her bed on the dais, silky waves of red hair spread over the soft pillows around her. Her plump cherry lips are slightly parted, her small nose flaring imperceptibly as she breathes in.

By God, she's so beautiful, like a Sleeping Beauty. The white silk gown flows like a milky river over her firm round breasts, sloping down her flat abdomen to her thighs. She has one knee up, the silk falling off her finely muscled leg.

"Nero, is everything all right?" The alarm in Drago's voice stirs me from my trance.

"Yes, I, yes."

He pauses. He must sense it in my voice. I realize I have the same dreamy voice he did when he first fell for Arianna.

"What the hell, Nero," he breathes. His tone betrays that he understands exactly what happened—that I have imprinted on a woman.

"Let's set the time for the meeting tomorrow. We'll talk about the rest when we're face to face, alone," I say.

It takes only a few moments to set the meeting, then I cut the call. I walk slowly to her bed, and lower myself on the edge.

Fuck me, will I ever get enough of this? Enough of staring at this woman? My heart fills with a strange kind of thirst that can only be satisfied by staring at her continuously, without even blinking. But there's also something else. There's... a strange kind of gentleness.

I raise my hand and trace her cheek as lightly as I would with the petal of a rose. She's so delicate, so fragile. And I put her through hell for months as I prepared my entry to Darkwood Falls City Hall, even if indirectly. I put her under pressure because I was certain she'd been hand in hand with Sullivan, the former mayor. I was wrong, now serpents' acolytes are after her, and I don't even want to imagine what they would have done to her if I hadn't stepped in tonight.

But I will find out, and I'll put them through whatever horror they had prepared for her. And then I'll skin them alive.

By God, her cheek feels like velvet under my rough finger that I never tried to use with so much gentleness before. I can't help it, and my thumb slips over her plump lower lip, feeling its hotness.

"Oh, God." I go dizzy with desire. I try to resist kissing her, but the wolf pushes, desperate for a taste of her. *She's sound asleep, she won't even know,* he growls.

I can't control myself and bend to her, closing my mouth over hers. My eyes shut slowly as my firm lips sink into hers, feeling the heat and softness. She stirs and moans, and I shoot back up only to realize I lost it, and my tongue slipped inside her mouth, greedy for more of her taste.

My gaze slides down her beautiful swan neck to her chest, her breasts, my hand moving just above the silk that caresses her body, along her belly down to her mound. God, how I'd love to be that silk. I want every inch of my big rough palms on this delicate white body, I want to push those finely muscled thighs apart and dip my rod of a cock in the cream of her arousal.

My brain swims in these feelings like in a sea of drugs. I let my powers loose, dulling Princess's mood in her sleep. If the sensations she feels on her body don't alarm her, she won't wake up. Our emotional connection has been building up ever since we made love, and now I can sense her in my flesh. That's how I know when she's entered the deepest phase of sleep.

The first thing I do is gently slip my hand under the silk gown, caressing my way up her inner thigh to her.... Oh wow. She didn't put any panties on after the bath she took. Could it be that she intended to make love to me again?

I wish she did. My fingers slide between her slick folds, and I inhale sharply as I realize my touch arouses her. She moans in her sleep, opening her thighs, inviting me to pleasure her with my hand. I sink one, then two thick fingers inside of her, feeling her hot slick inside sucking on them, pulling me in deeper. Fuck, she wants me, and that makes my cock ache to take her.

Yes, do take her, she's yours, the wolf demands, showing his fangs. It feels like the right thing to do, natural and good, but I shake my head, struggling to keep a clear mind. I can't just stick my cock inside this woman while she's sleeping, just because I feel entitled to. She has to agree, she has to want me.

But she gave herself to you tonight, the wolf insists. Yes, she did, but only because she had to, the drug that bastard put in her drink was going to kill her unless she got an orgasm. Whatever he had planned for her, she could have easily died. Many men think giving a woman an orgasm from her G-spot is easy, but it's not, and judging by what I felt from Princess, she hadn't had one before me. The look of utter ecstasy on her face, her widening eyes and her gaze up to the stars like the heavens had just opened up can only mean one thing—she had no idea such sensations existed until that moment.

Elation goes through me. I'm special to her, too, even if only in this little way.

She stirs, opening her legs wider. I swallow hard as she fully reveals the pink folded flesh between her legs, my fingers sunken inside of her, my knuckles glistening with her cream.

My cock aches, desperate for release. I pop the buttons of my fly open and free my erection, grabbing it with one hand while pumping Princess with the other. I'm gonna give us both pleasure at the same time, without actually taking her, I keep telling myself, but as I go on I want more. I need to feel her, even if only a little. She gave herself to me tonight, and she quivered in my arms as she came, she wouldn't mind if I just rubbed myself against her folds, would she?

I ease my fingers out of her only long enough to throw off my jeans, now standing fully naked beside her bed. Her white cheeks have caught that delicious red of arousal, her lips even redder, her lashes curved beautifully.

With my eyes glued to her, I crawl onto the bed over her, the soft mattress sinking and creaking under my weight, but Princess is fast asleep. She has to be having an erotic dream, and a pang of jealousy pierces my heart—who is she dreaming about? Is it me, is it us?

I sink a hand in her hair, keeping my weight on my elbows. My face is an inch above hers, and my lids fall heavy as I breathe in her scent. A feeling engulfs me like a drug—this is my woman, mine alone, and no one will ever take her away from me. Even if I can't show her how I feel, for so many reasons, she is mine.

I kiss her deeply, rocking my hips and sliding my cock between her folds. It's driving me insane, and I crave more. Both my hands sink in her hair, cupping her head, my tongue taking possession of her mouth as if making up for the fact that I can't enter her with my cock.

She moans and squirms under me, and I break the kiss, realizing I'm not letting her breathe. Fuck, I'm being a beast. My need for her is much too powerful, I've been squeezing her to my chest, crushing her fragile body under a wall of muscles.

There's some space between my torso and hers now, but I keep grinding my cock against her soft slick folds, dying to take her. Her perfectly arched eyebrows quiver as she whispers something.

"Nero, ah, yes, Nero."

I stop, my heart slamming against my chest. That was my name. She's having an erotic dream about me.

Take her, my wolf urges, using the euphoria now spreading through my body. *She wants it as badly as you do, why deny yourself?*

No, I can't. I can't take her without her knowledge. But she pushes her hips up to me, her body begging me to keep grinding when I've stopped, and the craving becomes uncontrollable. My struggle to resist only draws out the wolf, my skin burning and hardening, my eyes glowing, fur sprouting all over me.

Run, I have to run. The wolf has taken over, and he'll have me plunge my cock inside of her. *Yes, fuck her hard, she's yours, she's your fated mate, it's your birthright,* the beast pushes. But we live in a civilized world, and women have options. *My* woman is entitled to her options, and I won't take her without specific permission even if it kills me.

Thinking to force myself to get out of here, my eyes snap to the window, where they meet their own glowing golden reflection, and what looks like a scene from the '92 Dracula movie with the beast between the legs of the beautiful redhead, hungry for her. All my muscles tense as I get ready to leap out through the window, running out into the wild, but her legs clench around me.

"Nero," she sighs, lifting her hips from the bed. One glance down at where she rubs her slick pussy against my cock is enough to make me almost cum, growling deep from my chest. I grip my cock, keeping it in.

"Take me, Nero," she pleads, and I feel how she connects to me.

It's the most shocking feeling I've ever had. It's like all the cells of our bodies send energies that lace with each other, our brains forming an open network. I'm inside her dream, in which I'm taking her in my wolf form.

I could fight my own craving, but I'm hopeless against hers. In her dream she grabs my hips and guides me in. She doesn't touch me now, but I follow her dream and enter her, pushing her slick walls apart inch for inch.

My fangs piece my lower beast lip, my hands coiling around her wrists as I push her hands above her head. It's hard enough to keep from cumming as it is, if she touches me I'll fill her with my seed immediately, and it's important that she climaxes first. Right now, I exist only to pleasure her.

I drive my cock inside her pussy, trying hard not to growl. This house is big, but the sensations this woman gives me are through the roof, and I might become so loud that the windows quiver.

She moves to meet me, our bodies tangling with each other, quickly finding common rhythm. The dark windowpane reflects the scene, a beast ravishing a princess in a bed on a dais, while the Princess traps him between her long white legs.

She moans, pushing her head into the pillow, her wrists straining against my grip, and I can't hold it in anymore. I pull out of her before I cum, but I cum hard, driving my fangs into my lower lip until I taste blood to keep from growling. Drago lost his head and poured himself inside Arianna the first time they made love, when he imprinted on her, and she got immediately pregnant. The situation with Princess is much more complicated. She'd hate me to death if I left my sperm in her, and with good reason.

I cum all over the shiny silk on her belly, marking her as mine. I stroke my cock, delighted to the heavens as I watch my seed splash all over Princess. *My* woman, *my* mate.

I fall on the bed by her side, transforming back into a human, and relishing the taste of happiness that making love to her left on my tongue. I trace her hot flushed cheek with my finger, then let it slide down her red locks. Her eyes move slow under her closed eyelids, and she breathes deeply in and out.

"Nero," she whispers sweetly, turning to her side, now facing me.

The need to kiss her sweet red lips overwhelms me. I wind my arm around her, pulling her close to me, now fully a man, large and naked, holding his Sleeping Beauty. She curls with her check pressing to my chest, her hand caressing my side, her fingertips stroking hard muscle. My fated mate, the woman I imprinted on, caresses me lovingly in her dreams, unaware that it's happening in reality as well.

Just a few more minutes and then I'll get out of her bed, I tell myself, breathing in the perfume of her hair, and caressing her cheek. The rhythm of her breathing slows down as she sinks into a dreamless sleep, her warm breasts crushed against my body.

The sensation is like rivulets of bliss flowing through my veins instead of blood, so peaceful that I fall asleep. When I wake up, it's to Princess's bewildered caramel eyes above mine.

Oh, fuck. How do I explain now?

Nero

PRINCESS LOOKS AROUND at the ravished, torn sheets, taking a hand to her head. Her hair is messy, and her silk gown sticky with my cum.

"What the hell happened?"

"I, I—" What can I possibly say? I took her last night, made myself master of her body. I tapped into her dream, and I followed the instructions of her fantasies, but I won't use that to justify my actions. She didn't specifically permit me to make her mine.

I get off the bed, standing naked in front of her, my head down.

"Last night, after I secured the perimeter, I turned around, and found you asleep. I just couldn't.... I lost control. I tried to stop myself, I swear I did. I wanted to leap out the window, but right at that point you called my name repeatedly."

"You—"

"It's no excuse, and I'm not using it as one." I square my shoulders and look out the window into the sunrise, a soldier at her disposal. "Punish me as you see fit, Princess Skye. I gave in to my animal instincts and possessed you without your specific permission. It's an unforgivable sin, and I'll take whatever punishment you wish to give me, no matter how harsh. I would ask you not to have my life, though, the pack still needs me, and Darkwood Falls as well."

"Have your life," she whispers. The bewilderment and softness of her tone gives me the strength to look into her eyes. "I wouldn't take anyone's life, for whatever reason, but that you should be willing to let yourself be killed..." There are tears in her eyes. I connect to her, and realize she's crying because she's overwhelmed with positive emotion.

I sit down slowly by her side, reveling in our connection, still stark naked. I wipe a tear off her cheek with one finger, taking it to my lips and tasting it. I do it like a man in a trance, and the moment I feel that salty taste on my tongue, my mind starts to spin. I close my eyes, letting the taste run deep to my core, and I feel exactly what she feels.

Fuck. Me.

I'm sucked in the depths of Princess' feelings, realizing she's falling in love with me. Bliss and panic pull me out of that state, and my eyes snap open. I jump up to my feet, staring down at her in awe. I'm overwhelmed, with no idea what to say,

Princess shakes her head, laughing. It's the laugh of someone who can't believe what's happening.

"Nero, yesterday morning I thought you hated my guts. And now, look at us. We slept with each other twice, and you're offering me your life for.... I don't even know for what."

"I took you without asking permission. I'm—" It sounds terrible, but it's the truth. "I'm a rapist."

"You wouldn't have taken me if I didn't want you to. You said I called out your name, and I admit I was having an erotic dream about us, so...."

Color flushes in her cheeks and she looks down, her messy hair falling to hide her face from me. All I want is to reach under her chin and make her look up, but I have to refrain. I've done enough 'making' her do things.

"And what happens now?" She whispers. "Between us, I mean. Where do we stand?"

That question wrenches my heart.

The answer is simple, and yet I can't bring myself to say it. Taken with the sweetness of her love, I didn't stop to consider all the responsibility that comes with being the Alpha of my pack. A pack that depends on me, hell, all the werewolves on this side of the country depend on me, and the danger of the serpents is huge. Imprinting on a woman couldn't have happened at a worse moment.

With a sigh, I accept that I can't give Princess what she desires, because she'd be a distraction I can't afford. I have to suppress my own cravings and break both of our hearts.

Princess

HIS SILENCE IS ALL the answer I need. I still don't look at him, but direct my gaze to the window, to the now glowing sunrise. I can't let him see the tears of betrayal in my eyes.

"Is the perimeter safe then?" I try to keep my voice steady, but I don't think I'm fooling anyone, sure as hell not Nero.

"It is. I have people in place to guard the premises, and I'll send some in through the secret passageways, if that's all right. I'll use the plans you gave me. Does anyone else live in this house besides you and your father?"

"Two servants."

He gets dressed, I can hear him throwing his clothes on even though I'm not looking. Damn, I can still feel his cum sticking to my skin, gluing my gown to my body in multiple places. He came all over me like I was his dirty whore, but no man in his right mind would start an actual relationship with a woman he sees as such, right? Especially not the Alpha of a werewolf pack, a large, incredible hunk who can have any woman he wants. Indeed, why choose one when you could have many.

But I'll make him pay. Rage gives me the strength to smile, and turn my face to him. When our eyes meet, the handsome beast that is Nero Wolf seems taken aback. Sure, the bastard was expecting to see a hurting woman, probably a crying one, or maybe he expected that I would cling to him.

No, Sir. One thing I have left, and that is my dignity.

"Thank you again for saving my life last night," I say in a clear, crystalline voice. "And for the bonus orgasms you gave me in my sleep. I don't see any reason for punishment, and I wish you a nice life."

I get out of bed and walk to the bathroom.

"That's it?" Nero calls behind me. "That's all you have to say?"

"The fate of Darkwood Falls is in your hands, Mr. Mayor." At least I'm good at faking indifference, even if not at actually feeling it. "If there's anything I can do to help, give me a call, it's that easy. Wish you all the luck in the world catching the bad guys."

He follows me into the bathroom, probably bewildered that I actually look forward to the rest of my life even if he won't be in it.

"I don't understand your goodbye, Princess. We'll be working together at the City Hall, so we'll be seeing a lot of each other," he decrees as I turn on the water, strip and step into the shower.

I turn around, exposing my body fully to him, leaning my head back to let the water soak my hair.

"I can't hear you anymore, I'm sorry. But in case you said something about me working for you at City Hall, my resignation stands."

Just as I begin rinsing shampoo on my hair Nero turns off the hot water. Despite the shampoo that crawls to my eyebrows and threatens to slip into my eyes, I look into his angular, dangerous face, and shivers run through me. Fuck, the man is impressive, standing so close, and I want him again. I'm afraid the longer he stays, the less I'll be able to resist him.

"Princess, you can't be so blind to the danger you're in." He slides a muscular arm around my wet lower back, yanking me close. Fuck, I'm creaming for him.

"Yesterday, a serpent acolyte put something in your drink that could have *killed* you," he stresses. "I can't be very relaxed about that story, and neither should you. Look, I know that I promised the women of Darkwood Falls freedom, but in order for me to deliver on that promise I need you to work with me now, Princess. Darkwood Falls is in danger from the serpents, and you experienced this first hand. You can't just turn your back on this."

I place my hands on his chest, trying to push him away, but he keeps me close. Jesus Christ, the way those golden eyes glow, like he's about to shift any second. It hits me—did he take me in wolf form last night, like I dreamt he did? If so, I fucking loved it.

"If you don't do it for yourself, do it for the other women of Darkwood Falls," he insists, low and dark. "Arianna may have found her happiness with Drago, but what about the other girl I hear you care so much about? Janine, the owner of the hotel where I'm staying? What will become of her? You'd let her be alone for the rest of her life?"

That's like a slap in my face, one that wakes me up to reality, reminding me this isn't only about me.

"No, never, of course not," I breathe. "All right, I'll help."

Nero's hold on me loosens, but my arousal remains. His scent of wild woods and man is doing nasty things to me, and I'm afraid I'll fall down to my knees and take his cock in my mouth right here right now.

"Let us talk about this later." I manage to free myself from his hold. "This is hardly the place, and I'm not dressed for the occasion." I look down at my naked body. The way he eyes me up and down, full of desire, isn't lost on me, and it makes my heart jump with satisfaction. At least he wants me.

"The office then, City Hall," he says.

"I doubt we'll be able to talk about it there, there are eyes and ears everywhere. The Council isn't to be trusted either."

He smiles. "Then later? Somewhere private?"

Goose bumps rise all over my body, which is embarrassing. I brace myself.

"If I am to help you, give me the time to investigate. I'll need a few days, if not weeks, to do my research at City Hall. I'll let you know as soon as I have something worthwhile. Until then, we'll have to keep our interaction strictly professional while there. The Council are all hawks and hyenas, and the walls have their ears, so we can't touch any sensitive subject there."

"All right. Just so you know, I'll be staying at Janine's hotel. Drago says the place is as safe as it gets, and we hold our meetings with the entire pack there. When the time comes, let us meet there."

"All right then."

He makes to leave, and I turn on the water again, but then he turns around.

"If you ever go out in the evenings, I'll need to know when, where, and with whom. After what happened tonight, I don't think you'd still like to protest, or would you?"

I press my lips together in frustration. "No. What I'd like to do, though, is find out why those men put a sex drug in my drink. It doesn't make sense, it's a puzzle."

"We will find out, I promise. But, until then, keep me posted."

Before he turns to leave, I say, "I'm taking my dad to a business meeting with Lord Theodore Fritz tonight." I look behind me at him, feeling like I owe him an explanation. "My dad has been in a wheel chair for many years, and I'm the only one he trusts to take him to business meetings and keep his secrets."

Nero's handsome features tense. "I have a feeling that Theodore prick is in with the serpents. I can't be sure, but maybe you can get something out of him tonight, however small, a hint or a clue."

"Sure I can."

Theodore is into me, he always has been. But I suppose I can't tell Nero that, even though he wouldn't care. He might actually send me to suck the sleazy prick's cock in order to milk him of information, but I can't dwell on that right now, or I'm going to cry.

"Now, if you don't mind." I turn my back to him and turn the water on, closing my eyes and letting the rapid drops cover my face. I don't want him to see I'm falling apart from the inside. From now on, Nero Wolf will only see the strong side of me.

CHAPTER IV

Princess

Theodore Fritz's house is as creepy as the man himself. From the moment the big iron gates open, screeching like scarecrows, until I've finally pushed Dad's wheelchair into the large dark dining room, the place has given me the chills.

It's just a feeling, though, and I know it. Theodore Fritz is no supernatural creature. I mean, look at him. He's dressed in a bright blue sheen suit that's just not right for him, and he's a bit hunchbacked under it from all the ass kissing he's done all his life. He's actually a young man, barely in his fifties, but there's something about him that makes him seem spent. He's led a life of decadence that's taken a toll on him.

"Ah, Charles, old friend, so good to finally have you in this house after so much time."

"Thank you for the invitation," Dad replies in his gritty voice, but his tone betrays he's not here for pleasure. He doesn't like Theodore, he never has.

I bring Dad's wheelchair to Theodore's side, and then walk behind our host's chair to sit on his left. A tall, thin and grim-looking valet holds my chair for me and, as I lower myself in it, I look fully into Dad's face.

It's one of the few occasions when I can see his face clearly, thanks to the candles. For years he's been keeping to his chambers, withdrawing to the dark whenever I went to see him. Now that I think about it, I don't think we've eaten at the same table in years. When Mom's home, I mostly eat with her, and she's a talker, so I haven't really felt his absence. I've grown accustomed to it, I guess, or maybe the big picture of him dominating above the fireplace in the dining room made up for it. But now I fully understand why he avoids being seen.

His skin looks like it's falling off his face. My heart breaks for him, and my chin trembles. I blink away the tears, trying hard not to get emotional, but just look at him, my poor daddy. For all his money, nothing can save him from this decay. Luckily the medication he gets from Arianna's R&D labs keeps him alive and pain-free, but is that a good thing? Having him in this world is a blessing to me, but now I wonder if it's not more of a curse to him, if he wouldn't be better off without.

I pick up my glass of wine, on Theodore's invitation.

"It's an old burgundy, I'm sure someone of refined taste such as yourself will appreciate it."

I stop with the glass at my mouth, remembering yesterday. There could be anything in it.

"Don't," I yelp, and Dad's dry hand with the protruding old veins stops an inch from his mouth.

Theodore's puzzled face turns to me.

"Why not, my dear?" His parched lips pull in a grin that reveals crooked teeth. "Surely, you wouldn't suspect I'd poison the two of you, do you?"

I lift my chin like a lady, glass of wine in hand.

"Poison? Now why would I suspect *that*, Lord Fritz?" I make just a short pause to assess the look on his face that seems to draw longer, but then I continue. "My father is permanently on medication, and the doctors insist that he should avoid alcohol. It might meddle with the chemistry, you see."

It may be just in my head, but I think a shadow of disappointment falls over Theodore's face.

"My daughter is right, Theodore," Dad says, his voice even grittier. Talking is causing him more trouble as the months go by. He places the glass on the table, keeping his long dry fingers on the stem.

"Not a problem, Charles. More for Princess and me," Theodore jokes.

"Actually." I put the glass down, too. "I had a bit of a rough night, and I don't think alcohol is a good idea for me either." I splay my hand over my chest where Theodore's eyes are slipping as I speak, covering most of my cleavage. I'm wearing a red shiny dress that clings to the shape of my body. "To my defense, I must say it was the new mayor's fault. I was so mad at him forcing me to stay in his service that I had to calm down somehow. I must admit I may have had too much to drink."

I watch carefully for Theodore's reactions. The more I look at him, the less I trust him. Must be something in his body language that just doesn't sit well with me. Still, my distrust may also have to do with the way he amassed his wealth, which includes driving companies into bankruptcy, and shady dealings with the government. Not to mention the rumors that his main area of expertise back in his youth was espionage.

"Well, first of all, he is *new*. He's not even from Darkwood Falls. I mean, what do we even know about him?"

"Nero Wolf's presence in Darkwood Falls is a scandal and a threat, Theodore," Dad says.

My eyes snap to him over the table. This is backwards. I expected Dad to be afraid of Sullivan's revenge, I mean, he was terrified of murder attempts these past months. I expected that he'd actually seek an alliance with the new mayor, not spit fire as soon as I mention him.

"His taking over City Hall is the main reason why I wanted to see you. We have to get rid of the Wolf brothers, and fast."

"Wait, let's take this calmly," Theodore says, putting up his palm. "First of all, he is an interim mayor, chosen by the Council. There will be elections in six months, and I don't think Nero Wolf actually stands a chance. I don't even think he's interested in running."

"Yes, but even for an interim mayor, why *him*? There were so many people in Darkwood Falls who could have filled the position," Dad insists as the valet places a bowl of steaming soup in front of me.

"The problem is exactly that, Charles—the people of Darkwood Falls and their broken trust." Theodore hunches over his own soup, elbows on the table, and begins spooning to cool it. "After what happened with Sullivan, him taking off like that with half of the elite's money, people don't trust local candidates anymore, especially the elite. Some members of the Council demanded that we bring in someone that would fulfill special conditions—impossible conditions, if you ask me. The interim mayor had to be both local and outsider, old money, but also young and powerful, having proven him-or herself to the entire country, not just this town. That's when Arianna Parker's new—" He looks at me with a fake question in his eyes. "What is he even to her, husband, lover? He is the father of her babies, we know that, but what exactly is the nature of their relationship?"

I jut out my chin. "He's her husband." Theodore's mouth pops open, which fills me with satisfaction. He didn't expect there was a wedding that he wasn't invited to. Eat this, prick. "They got married in secret because they didn't want to make a fuss in these times of turmoil for Darkwood Falls. Like you said, Sullivan took off with a great deal of the elite's money, people have other priorities now."

Theodore returns his attention to Dad. "Yes, well he is one charismatic chump, that Drago Wolf, isn't he? He argued he is now a local, even if his older brother Nero isn't, but he recommended Nero because he fulfilled all the other conditions."

Dad's eyes are still blazing, and Theodore leans closer with a secret. He looks sleazy as he does that. Probably because he plays loyal to Nero at City Hall, but in truth he's a snake waiting to bite.

"It's not like I don't understand your worries, old friend. But if we are to kick the Wolf brothers out of Darkwood Falls, we'll have to be strategic about it."

"Strategic how?"

"You'll see next Saturday. I have a plan."

"Like I said, I didn't like Nero Wolf from the start," I chime in, spooning through my soup. "I'd like nothing more than to see him go."

"You will see him go Princess, I promise you that. You could even help make that happen, you know? You could stay in his service as mayor's assistant, and try to find his weaknesses. Things that we can use against him in case he wants to make his stay here longer than planned."

"What if he doesn't have weaknesses or dirty secrets?"

Dad and Theodore burst into laughter. Dad even chokes on it and reaches for a glass of water with a trembling hand. I hurry and bend over the table to push it closer to him. The sleazy way that Theodore's eyes slip down my exposed cleavage isn't lost on me either.

"No man wielding as much power and money as Nero Wolf can ever be completely clean, Princess," Dad explains. "I thought you learned as much after twenty-seven years in the world of the rich." His voice becomes drier with every word, and he sips his water at the end of the sentence.

"I have learned quite a bit. For example, I've learned that men as powerful as you and Theodore would never have let a man take the mayor's chair without knowing everything there is to know about him. Why don't you share that information with me, it would be a good starting point, at least it would give me an idea where to start looking for weaknesses and secrets."

"Oh, we have information," Theodore says, returning to his soup. "But unfortunately it only tells us how powerful the man is."

"He's got fantastic PR," Dad chimes in. "And he knows how important it is to build an image as someone who's as good as indestructible. It gives people trust." His eyes glint. "We will give you key data, but you must promise us something, Princess."

"Anything."

"That you won't let this man's power seduce you. You have to be strong, because Nero Wolf is not a man easy to resist. He has more money than a sheik, more power than the Russian president, and the looks of cover model. Few women can resist that kind of allure."

"We actually have most of our information from scorned women." Theodore laughs. I try to control my reactions as he talks, but my cheek won't stop trembling.

"Nero Wolf is the eldest of five brothers, you know that," Theodore begins. "Their parents were murdered when the boys were little, but they left a huge inheritance behind. The boys were raised in an orphanage until Nero came of age, and took over his parents' business, but by that time there wasn't much left of it. The heads of the orphanage had squandered everything."

"But they still had the family name and the contacts," Dad picks up when Theodore stops to start on the steak. "Nero was very good at sciences, a kind of genius, and he proved very talented on Wall Street. But." Dad's gaze darkens, and the entire room seems to darken with it.

"He couldn't get the companies out of so much debt, they were in too deep. Soon after this became apparent, his financial advisors tried to persuade him to sell what he could. But then the strangest thing happened. The headmasters of the orphanage where he and his brothers had grown up were all found dead in the headmaster's office, slaughtered as if beasts had torn them apart. And guess what? All those men had signed the money they had stacked in the Cayman Islands away to Nero just days before they died. Now isn't that one pretty coincidence?"

No, this can't be right. Nero has been alive for five hundred years, so he became of age centuries ago. He couldn't have killed the headmaster and the others in the day of Wall Street. This doesn't add up.

"They defied everyone, including the police," Theodore continues. "It was obvious the brothers were involved in the murders, but no one could prove it because the victims had been apparently torn apart by beasts."

"Like wolves," Dad mutters as he eats.

"That you should be able to tell me all this while you're eating," I breathe, fighting the returning lump in my throat.

"The brothers got away with the crime, just like that," Dad puts in. "The investigators soon closed the case."

I let all this go through my head. I knew about the orphanage, Drago told me the story. I know that the headmaster and teachers were cruel to the boys, whipped them and tormented them, purely out of hatred. Drago has a theory that they hated the rich, and took it out on them because they were the kids of rich people, now orphaned. But he never mentioned the slaughter. And, again, all that happened centuries ago, way before companies and Wall Street.

I clear my throat. "And how do you know all this?"

"Investigators and retired reporters who owe us favors," Theodore replies. "Better not get into the mechanics of it. But there are also things we found out from scorned women."

"What things?"

He grins with the promise of a surprise. "Come to my soiree next Saturday, and you'll find out. But here's a teaser—Nero Wolf had affairs with a number of high-born heiresses. He probably went for them because they had every reason to keep the liaison secret, and he didn't have to worry about unwanted publicity. He must have had hundreds of women in his life. As much as I hate to admit it, he is breathtakingly handsome."

"I didn't know you appreciated male beauty." Dad looks at Theodore darkly from under his eyebrows.

"On, don't worry Charles, I'm as straight as they come." One glance at me makes that obvious, in a deeply disturbing way. My skin crawls, but I manage to suppress a shudder. "I'm merely assessing the competition, so to say." He's the only one who laughs at his own joke.

"Well," he continues, returning to his steak, "he hurt those women. They fell in love with him, and crawled at his feet, but nothing helped. He refused to make any of those liaisons official." He looks at me with a warning. "The man is as cold-hearted as he is handsome, so don't let those fallen angel looks fool you."

The memory of Nero naked by the side of my bed comes to mind, tall and broad-shouldered, sculpted as a god, looking coldly down at me after a night of passion.

"I won't," I whisper.

"There was only one woman with whom he had a longer arrangement," Theodore continues, making a point. "Paola Valdez, a fiery Latina heiress. She moved to Spain at some point, and only came back to the US recently. What is it, honey, something stuck in your throat?"

I realize I'm staring at Theodore clutching my fork and knife, probably making a face.

"No. No, I'm okay, please go on." But my blood is boiling under my skin. I look down to avoid Dad's questioning scowl.

"Paola's theory is that Nero Wolf had more than just sexual interest in her, because he visited every night and he mostly didn't even want, well, you know, sex. She was pretty sure of herself when she—"

"How long ago were they together?" Damn it, my lips are so tight that I'm speaking through my teeth.

"About five years, Paola said." He leans over to me, a bad smell coming from his mouth. "But if you want details you'll get the chance to ask her yourself. You're going to meet her at my soiree. I invited her."

"Well, I guess it's going to be quite a surprise for the mayor," I grunt past the lump in my throat.

"No, not really." Theodore resumes eating. "I mentioned the fact that I knew her to the mayor. Since Paola said they had been close, I figured I'd tell him, maybe having her as a common acquaintance would earn me a place in his confidence. He sat up, and asked me to invite her to Darkwood Falls. He's looking forward to seeing her again, if you ask me."

I shoot up to my feet, my chair scratching the floor. Both men stare at me surprised, especially Dad.

"I'm sorry," I manage.

I need to get out of here fast, before the Molotov cocktail of feelings inside me blows up, and both Theodore and Dad realize that I slept with the new mayor, and hoped for something more because I'm a complete idiot. But I can't use the ladies' room excuse, they'll see right through it.

"I promised I'd call Arianna about some papers tonight, and I totally forgot. I just remembered now that you mentioned heiresses and connections." I grab my clutch, manage a smile and make my way outside.

I run through the big, dark house like a ghost, looking for an exit. I find one to the back yard, and breathe in the crisp night air, letting it cool my heated face. I sit on a broken stair and bury my face in my palms, beating myself up for having been so stupid.

Sure, the intimacy I experienced with Nero Wolf was unique, out of this world, the orgasms he gave me on the hood of his car shook me to my core. The lovemaking from last night, which I'd thought only a dream, was a mystical experience, something almost tantric that I could grow addicted to. How could that mean so much to me and so little to him?

I remember his reserved attitude towards me this morning, making it clear there would be nothing more between us. God, how can he stay so cold after what we had? True, we barely know each other, but it feels like it's meant to be, and it can't be one sided, it just can't. But wait. Isn't this what all stalkers think? That they are meant to be with the object of their affection, only if this person would finally see that?

I raise my head from my hands and wipe the tears from my face. They keep coming, but it's only because I need the release. I'm growing stronger by the second and, by next Saturday when I'll get to watch him come face to face with this Paola Valdez, I'll be strong enough. I have to be. I have to remember he's had countless women, all of them willing to do anything to keep him as a lover—I can understand why, if he made love to them like he did to me. But I won't be one of the many falling at his feet, worshipping and adoring him. No Sir, not even if the desire for him burns me to death.

I drive Dad and me home, firm in my decision—I will stay in Nero's service. I'll dig deep to find out exactly what Sullivan was into, and why he sent his acolytes to put a sex drug in my drink.

As soon as I've closed the door to my room a feeling of emptiness engulfs me. I look around, remembering Nero in here yesterday, still feeling his presence. I change into a silk night robe and sit at the vanity table, staring at myself in the mirror and bracing myself.

"Look at you, Princess Skye," I murmur, tracing one porcelain-white cheek with my hand. "Missing the feel of his hot body on yours, his scent, his presence in this room as if you've been together for years. How stupid is that."

My hand drops off my face, but I keep staring at the white girl with the caramel eyes and long waves of red hair. For the first time ever, I have a moment of complete honesty with myself.

I'm a twenty-seven year old woman who still doesn't know who she is. I have never even really left Darkwood Falls except for fashion shows and a few adrenaline-pumping secret one-night stands. I eventually found a purpose in life by working at City Hall. Sullivan had become dependent on me for everything in his schedule and, even though I hated his guts, especially for what he'd done to Arianna, I felt useful. Working at City Hall made me feel needed and valuable, it made me feel good about myself.

In the silence I think I hear the heavy breathing of an animal outside my door, steady but deep, almost like muffled huffing. I walk slowly to the door, unsure whether to open it. Placing my palms on it, I remember that Nero has the place guarded in order to make sure Sullivan doesn't attack Dad or send his acolytes for me, but as far as I know he doesn't have werewolves here. Only well-trained, normal security men.

The huffing persists, as if someone is sniffing behind the door. I grip the doorknob, my pulse shooting up. Could it be?

Nero

I MAKE IT OUT JUST before Princess opens the door to her room. I couldn't control my need to feel her close, even for a little bit. I needed to at least breathe in her scent, a craving that drove me crazy. It drew me closer and closer until I pressed my cheek and my palms to her door, saying her name inside my head. Of course she felt me, she's now mine as much as I am hers.

I speed out of the manor, out into the dark back yard and into the woods. I leap over a thick fallen tree trunk, shifting in the air. I land on my huge paws, racing through the woods, wind and branches whipping by me.

I shift back in front of Drago's house, and climb in through the kitchen window. I sniff around to make sure Arianna doesn't catch me, because I'm stark naked. I shifted without thinking in the woods, all because of my maddening need for Princess, and my clothes tore apart in the process.

I sneak up to Arianna's and Drago's bedroom. I move too softly for any human's senses, but Drago is my brother, a werewolf, and he surely knew I was coming before I emerged from the woods. He's already on his feet and holding out a pair of jeans and a black fitted tee when we meet each other's eyes.

"Let's talk downstairs," he says, motioning for me to lead the way. He always needs to be the last in the room, protecting his wife who's carrying his two babies. He'd probably be with her twenty-four seven if he could, but he fears it would suffocate her.

"This could be you and Princess," he says as he turns on the light in the kitchen. "You should give in to what you feel, Nero, you'll never be able to fight it."

"I never imagined it would be this way. This ache for her, right here in my chest, it's tearing me apart." I lean with my palms on the counter, trying to cope with the feeling.

Drago opens the cupboard. "Need a drink?"

"The strongest you have."

Even though I can't see his face, I know he smirks.

"When you fell for Arianna," I say, turning around and taking the drink from him, "I thought I understood what you were feeling. I was wrong."

"One of your strong suits that prove you're a true leader—you know how to admit that you were wrong."

I down the brandy, the kind that I used to make for my brothers. The kind that can actually get a werewolf drunk, since normal alcohol is wasted on us.

"Don't sweat it." Drago leans against the fridge, facing me. Both his jeans and tee are tight on me, straining to snap, so I try not to move a lot. "You'll get Sullivan with her help in a couple of months max, then you'll be able to make your relationship official."

"No, Drago. We can't be together, now or ever."

Drago frowns, his intense dark eyes probing the feelings all over my face. "I don't understand. I sensed it clearly when we talked on the phone, and I can feel it now—you imprinted on her. Which means you—" He pauses, knowing better than to say 'you had sex with her'. Imprinting is so much more than that. "You merged with her."

"Physical intimacy isn't always necessary in order to imprint." I try to save the situation, for Princess's sake.

"Not always, but mostly. And I can smell her on you, Nero, so don't even try to deny it. You'll have to be completely honest with me, otherwise I can't help you. And you need all the help you can get right now."

"The ache in my chest is unbearable. I need her closeness as much as air."

"Yes, finding your mate can do that to you. If you're not with her, the feeling can destroy you from the inside out. But I don't understand, Nero, you know this better than anyone. Why do you keep yourself away from her?"

"I'm the Alpha of this pack, the werewolves depend on me. And not just our people, all the werewolves on this side of the country. I can't afford soft spots, weaknesses. Imagine the serpents finding out that I have found my mate, imagine what that would mean, especially for Princess."

Drago frowns, his intense eyes even darker. "They'd hunt her down for the rest of her life. They'd stop at nothing to get her, and use her against you."

"And let's look at the most probable scenario." I look the ugly truth in the face. "They'd kill her, weakening me to the point that I'd be useless. No werewolf can live after their fated mate is dead, not unless they have offspring. The grief over a mate is deadly for werewolves. Imagine what that would mean for the pack."

Drago's features harden as he mulls this over, but there's nothing he can say. There is no solution to this. It's not like werewolves can choose their alphas democratically, like humans do with their political leaders. We obey the laws of nature, the laws of the beast, and these laws choose the alpha. If an alpha dies, the pack stays behind weak and vulnerable, headless until nature provides a new one. One of my brothers would probably upgrade into an alpha after my death, but the process takes time, and during that time they would be easy prey for the serpents.

Drago and I look into each other's eyes, both understanding there's no solution to this other than me renouncing the love of my life. For both her sake and the werewolves'.

"You carry the weight of the world on your shoulders, big brother," Drago says. "What are you going to do?"

I shake my head. "I don't know."

"How does she feel about all this? Does she know you imprinted on her? Because let me remind you what that means—she won't be able to fall in love with another man either. She's bound to you for life."

"I just know I want her to live, and happily. You know, she confronted me about restricting her freedom, and not letting her date men from outside Darkwood Falls, just like the former mayor did. I explained to her why, but she was in a rage, and I understood her, truly. She'd been waiting for her chance at freedom for a long time, and now that she finally thought she'd be able to reach out and grasp it, the new mayor comes with the same restrictions as the old one. I explained to her why that is, but she wouldn't have it. That's why she went to a pub, got herself drunk, and men surrounded her like moths drawn to a flame." I ball my fists as I remember. "These feelings are going to kill me. I wish somebody else could feel what I do in my place."

"You'd kill anyone who did. If anyone ever comes on to Princess you'll lose your mind. It won't be easy, brother, keeping away from her. Especially if you insist on having her at City Hall."

"She can help us track Sullivan down."

"Yes, but the problem remains—how are you going to put up with having her so close, and not touch her, not make her yours every chance you get?"

"I'll be busy." I prepare inwardly before I give him the big news. "Paola Valdez is coming to town."

Drago grins. "Now that is interesting news."

CHAPTER V

Princess

It's hard, being around Nero. Knowing he's here, just behind the high baroque double doors to my left, while I sit at the desk in the antechamber. I admit that I'm wearing a low-cut silk green shirt with a push up bra from Victoria's Secret underneath especially to turn him on. Even though our encounters didn't mean half as much to him as they did to me, he enjoyed doing me, and I'll make him crave to do it again.

But he doesn't even look at me. Whenever I'm called inside to attend his meetings he's completely focused on them, and whenever we meet down in the City Hall cafeteria, where numerous employees roam around him, he keeps with his back at me. All I get is glimpses of his chiseled profile. God, how I long to feel those masculine carnal lips on mine at least one more time.

"Fuck this," I grunt under my breath, and strengthen myself in the decision to stop caring. He's going to see the one woman he ever had feelings for in only a few days at Theodore's soiree, so I might as well lose all hope.

I make an effort, and manage to focus on looking as deeply as possible into Sullivan's business. After hours of research I lean back with the salad I got from the cafeteria, immersed in thought. It's already after seven, the City Hall empty, and I can make myself comfortable.

If I were Sullivan, why would I have sent my acolytes to put a sex drug in my drink, and what would I have wanted to achieve by doing that? A possible answer comes to mind as I fall deeper into a state of half-meditation.

Maybe Sullivan wanted me out of the way before I could start discovering things about him and tell the werewolves. But murder would have made more sense than having his acolytes put a sex drug in my drink that would have killed me unless I had sex with somebody.

Then it hits me— Darkwood Falls is one of the very rare places in the world where Fated Females exist, the kind of females that werewolves can imprint on and have children with. Then I remember something of my past, something I dismissed many years ago. Of course, why didn't I think about it before?

I re-emerge to full awareness to find Nero standing in front of my desk. I slide the fork slowly out of my mouth, after the last mouthful of salad I've taken. I realize I must have eaten slowly, lost in thought.

"Waiting for someone, Miss Skye?" he inquires gruffly, his glowing golden eyes moving to my cleavage. I've loosened my shirt to make myself more comfortable, expecting I'd be alone. The upper sides of my green silk are gaping open, uncovering the lace trim of my black Victoria's Secret bra. My cheeks flush red with embarrassment, and I hurry to button up the shirt.

"I didn't expect you back, Mr. Mayor."

His eyes move up and down my body, but I can't tell whether it's with lust or anger.

"Well, it sure looks like you were expecting *someone*."

I look up at him, my cheeks burning with rage. "What are implying?"

"It's hard to believe you were licking the fork with your breasts half out expecting to be by yourself. Who was supposed to walk in and be impressed by the sight greeting him?"

I stare up at him standing there in his fitted black suit, looking huge and handsome. Those golden eyes pierce mine, demanding an explanation.

"Are you accusing me of having invited a lover to the office thinking you were gone for the night, is that what you're saying?"

His eyes blaze, his jaw set. He doesn't reply, but I read the rage in his face, and a feeling sweet as honey replaces my own anger— satisfaction. I'm tempted to let him believe that. And, considering the decision I made just before he snapped me out of my thinking trance, I might actually do it. I'll let him think I'm seeing someone— and this time he won't be able to stop me, because the guy is a local. Or used to be.

I gather my things, getting ready to go. "Tell you what. Why don't you wait for my supposed lover yourself? Find out who it is. Have a nice evening." I square my shoulders, clutching my stuff at my chest, looking him in the eyes as coldly as I can. "Mr. Mayor."

I walk around my desk, my heart thudding when I try to sidestep him. But he grabs my arm, forcing me to a halt, and when I look up into his face I'm sure I'll melt. He's looking at me with smoldering, bedroom eyes. I shake my head, certain I'm seeing only what I want to see. I try to jerk out of his grip, but he won't let me.

"I'll have you continue your research," he says in a low, rough voice. "I'll pay you for your extra hours."

"May I remind you I don't work here because I need the money. But because you asked for me help, and I agreed to give it."

Nero lets go of my arm but still stands in front of me, his scent of wild woods tantalizing my senses. I have to get away from him, and fast, before his presence gets me drunk and I fucking jump on him.

I turn on my heel and head out of City Hall so fast that I misstep a couple of times in my pumps, twisting my ankles. It's a miracle that I don't break them by the time I get to my Beetle, slam the door shut and press the ignition button.

Tears stream down my face as I drive home. It's not tears of sadness or any kind of hurt, though, it's tears of release. Nero's presence does weird things to me, as if every cell of my body connects to him, craves him. But I won't give in to that. I've heard many women insist they felt a connection to the man they stalked, justifying their clinging to him. I refuse to be one of those women.

Nero

THEODORE FRITZ'S MANOR glows from a distance. The scents of the crowd, booze and aperitifs hit me as I step out of the black car, the driver holding my door. I hate the feeling of being placed above others, and my mouth tightens the moment the first awestruck face meets mine.

There was a time when people treated my brothers and me like junk, back at the orphanage. Looked down on us like we were second-hand creatures, less than human. Now that same kind of entitled people move aside as I step inside the drawing room. They're the crème de la crème, all drinks and laughs, staring at me in fear and respect. But I'm not fooled. Times change, faces change, tradition and habits transform, but the psychology of these entitled bastards stays the same.

"Our honored Mr. Mayor," the host, Lord Theodore Fritz, greets. He spreads his arms widely as if welcoming an old friend, probably a way of establishing himself as someone who's in the mayor's confidence. One hug would be enough to place him on a pedestal, securing him a special position among the crème.

I'd probably even go along with it, make him feel safe so he can start making mistakes. I'm not above dirty strategies such as making him feel important, stroking his ego to get what I want from him. But there's one thing about him that activates the beast in me, shutting down my better judgment—he's into Princess.

So I stop in front of him, squaring my shoulders, towering over him. His eyes widen. The bastard can't believe I'm actually making him look bad in front of all these people, deliberately.

He decides to sidestep me and just begin the introduction, trying to save face.

"To those of you who haven't had the chance to meet our interim mayor, may I introduce—" He motions to me as if presenting an auction item. "Mr. Nero Wolf."

Drago and Arianna come forth, the small woman with the face of an angel heavily pregnant. They proposed and vouched for me as mayor, and most of the elites here accepted to support me because I run multinational businesses that they want to at least dip their fingers in. And because of my influence that reaches even the Congress.

Having me as mayor was a huge opportunity for them, and they didn't even have to give me Darkwood Falls for good. I'm just the interim mayor, and the bastards think they'll get something compromising on me before the six months are over, forcing me to support them even if I don't win the elections. Too bad I've been in this game for too long, and I know every trick in the book.

I make small talk with some of the elites, Drago and Arianna at my side, Theodore watching the whole time. He approaches me when he gets the chance, whispering in my ear.

"You made me look bad in front of all these people, Mr. Mayor. I'd like to know what I've done to deserve that. I've supported you from the beginning, haven't I? I even got your long lost girlfriend here."

"And I appreciate the support, Lord Fritz. But you tried to force my hand into creating a certain image for you, without having discussed it with me beforehand. I don't appreciate being used."

"I never complained about *you* using *me*, have I?"

"I never used you for free. I always paid you for your favors." I turn to the side, looking down at the hunched man that looks like a hyena. "Or are you dissatisfied with the amount?"

"Nero," a familiar woman's voice calls. I turn around and recognize the naturally tanned face of Paola Valdez.

She stalks over to me, the crowd moving out of her way. She's wearing at least twenty grand of designer clothes and accessories, her long, thick hair the color of walnut tumbling in styled waves around her. She's got the same dark eyes and fixed gaze full of ambition, but devoid of depth.

Paola is a woman who lives for money and power. Many admire her for it, but they don't know what I do—Paola is an emotional cripple. She can't love anyone because she's not equipped to. As for men, they're just a means to an end, even if those ends are mostly orgasms.

I bend down just enough to let her put her hands on my shoulders, reluctantly touching my cheek to hers as she air kisses me.

"What a fantastic surprise," she says with a bleached grin.

"Paola, good to see you. I didn't know you were back in the States."

"I returned a few months ago."

I smile and look down, avoiding her eyes that burn with desire already. She was always a visual woman, quick to light up for what she considered a good-looking male. I would use that to get information out of her, but she'd want to fuck in return, and I can't be with her anymore. Not after I had Princess, it would tear the heart out of me.

We catch up for a while until Theodore leaves our side and goes on to welcome newcomers. I catch a glimpse of Princess somewhere in a group, and my whole body reacts.

"Looking for someone?" Paola asks as I crane my neck for Princess.

"Just thought I saw someone I know."

She slips an arm around mine. "Surely not someone you haven't seen in years, like me. I would have expected to have all of your attention, at least for tonight."

There's reproach behind her fake smile.

"Of course."

She nudges my side, and I wind an arm around her shoulders. She's wearing stilettos, but she's still quite small compared to me.

"So how come you never called? Or come to visit me in Spain?" Honey glazes the reproach in her tone.

"You know how it is for me, always busy. The business, now political engagements. But I'm glad you came back. Too bad I had to find out from Theodore."

"Oh, don't be upset. Like I said, I haven't been back long, and I had to see to the family business first. Then Theodore contacted me, saying you were going to take over City Hall in Darkwood Falls, and that meant you were finally showing your face to the world." She stops in place, making me do the same. "I have to admit, I decided to make a grab for you. You weren't ready for a relationship five years ago, maybe something's changed now?"

"I'm still a player and a bad boy."

She laughs out loud. "You never were. If anything, you were too serious. But if your stone heart is ready to be melted, I'm right here with the right kind of flame."

Princess appears in my field of vision, and my eyes sharpen. My entire body tenses, and I can even feel the pupils of my eyes expand. I know that Paola follows the direction of my stare, but I can't control myself.

I can't tear my eyes away from the beauty in the long red dress that hugs her fairy-like body. I'm dying to touch that porcelain skin, her long beautiful swan neck she exposes when she tilts her head to the side, smiling at someone. My eyes focus like a hawk's to see who she's smiling at, and fire roars in my heart—it's Theodore Fritz's young nephew, also visiting. Theodore introduced him to me when I arrived.

Ramses Fritz smiles with all he's got at Princess. It's obvious he's delighted to be around her, and a thousand questions shoot through my head—how long have they known each other, how familiar are they, did they use to play together as kids, or are they each other's teenage crush?

I could spit fire the moment his arms wind around her, her bare back tightening as his long fingers splay over it.

"You know the girl?" Paola tries to slip her hand into mine, and I realize it's balled in a fist.

"She's my secretary."

"And you wish she were more than that?"

"No," I grunt the lie. "I'm watching her because I don't trust her. I think she was in on the former mayor's shady business, and that's the only reason I keep her around. I need to get my hands on all of Sullivan Haan's secrets, if I'm ever to free this town of him."

"Speaking of that, what is special about this town? Why settle down here?"

"My brother lives here now, with his wife. They're expecting twins."

"Which one of your hunky brothers got married?" She frowns up at me. As far as she knows my brothers are too wild to settle for one woman, so this must come as a huge surprise.

"Drago."

"What?" she yelps. "Of all the people in the world, Drago Wolf? The cage fighter and ladies' man?"

I shrug. "He found the right lady."

I can see the envy cross her eyes. She was always into me the most, but I know she would have taken whichever one of us she could get her hands on.

"To be completely honest, I never thought I'd ever see any of your brothers married. You're all breathtakingly handsome, rich, powerful, you have so many women at your feet it's actually a shame that you should settle for one."

"Like I said, she is Miss Right for him. They fell deeply in love."

"So that's why you took over City Hall as interim mayor? For them?"

"I think this town can become a home for my family, yes. I like it. The mountains, the woods, the falls, the wild. It suits us."

She smiles. "Indeed. So, you're interim mayor now, are you going to run for the job in six months?"

"I am. And many of the town's elites are going to support me, because Sullivan took off with a lot of their money, and they know I can help them get it back."

Paola looks around with her ambitious little eyes, assessing the crème de la crème. "You might not need his former secretary for all that. I could help you track down Sullivan Haan."

I turn to her, pretending to be surprised. "You know him?"

"Not only do I know him, I've done business with him, too. I actually expect him to contact me soon for more."

Jackpot. Even if she doesn't take me all the way down to Sullivan's core secrets, she can surely point me in the right direction. And, most of all, she can help me understand why Sullivan sent serpent acolytes to put a sex drug in Princess's drink, a drug that would have even killed her if she didn't mate.

But in order for all that to work, I'll have to pretend that she, Paola, is the center of my attention, at least tonight.

Nero

I FAIL MISERABLY AT making Paola feel she's at the center of my attention. I follow Princess around as if my eyes are glued to her, and not only Paola notices. No matter who approaches me and tries to make conversation my eyes stay focused on her, even as I speak to them.

I know Princess can sense me stalk her like a mad man, she glances over her shoulder often. Every time her caramel eyes find mine crazy sensations run all over my skin. The wolf is agitated, sensing his mate, and dying to possess her. But he can't, and therefore he demands to shift, to sprint out into the woods and howl his devastating need up at the moon.

Paola grabs my forearm, taking me away from the group we're with at the moment.

"All right," she says in a no-nonsense tone as she draws me in an alcove. "I know you much too well, and you can't tell me that woman is just your secretary. Not even that all you want is to use her to track down Sullivan."

"I assure you that's all there is. She's not even my type."

Paola looks at Princess. "Tall, queenly, red hair and white skin, quite extravagant. Indeed, you were never into women who stand out like the morning star, but this one turns every head in the room. Yours the most. Even now, look at you. You can't tear your eyes away from her even when confronted about it."

For the first time in my life, I have no idea what to say. Paola cornered me, and there's no way I can deny that I'm drooling over this woman, hell, that right now I'm dying to follow her down the corridor where she disappeared with Ramses Fritz.

"Paola Valdez, is that you?" Drago appears from behind her, holding out his hand, his dark eyes simmering on his seductive bad boy face. She smiles widely in response, opening her arms to greet him, but Arianna's heavily pregnant stomach appears by his side, followed by Arianna herself.

The smile disappears from Paola's face.

"Wonderful to see you," she addresses Drago, watching for a look of jealousy on Arianna's face as she puts her hands on Drago's shoulders. To my delight, all she finds is a well-meaning smile. My sister-in-law knows all too well her man is only hers, hell, he wouldn't be able to sleep with another woman if he wanted to. He's obsessed with her, in the same way that I'm growing obsessed with Princess.

I'm relieved Drago stepped in, and he probably did it because he saw the predicament I was in. He has superhuman hearing, so he must have heard Paola, noticing at the same time that I'm at a loss. But instead of using the chance to pull myself back together and find a way out of this, I brush off my suit jacket, ball my fists, and stomp my way to the corridor where I saw Ramses Fritz take Princess.

I walk deeper into the manor, following her scent up the stairs. The deeper I go the emptier the manor gets, and the more I realize I might discover them in an intimate situation.

By the time I reach the chamber where their smell leads me I must look like a dragon breathing out flames. I clench my fists harder, ready to knock my way through concrete with my knuckles if I have to. But the door is ajar to one small chamber in the attic, a slip of orange light licking the rug, shadows moving inside.

Part of me doesn't want to push that door and see behind it, but the beast growls. My wolf fangs grow and I can't control the transformation. I'm way too angry.

I move as stealthily as ever when on the hunt only thanks to all my centuries of experience as a predator, but in truth I've never felt so insecure. I reach out and push the door, discovering Princess with her back at me. Fine muscles move underneath her perfectly white skin, her red hair sleek and nicely done on top of her head. I watch that elaborate hairdo move from side to side as she inspects the files stacked together on a higher shelf, perched on a small library ladder. The young Ramses Fritz stands by her side, gazing up at her full of longing, thinking no one can see him.

Relieved that she's not in his arms, kissing him, I push the door open all the way and walk inside. Princess whips around, falling off the ladder right into the young man's arms.

"Nero," she yelps. "I mean, Mr. Mayor."

"Mr. Wolf." Ramses' big brown eyes widen.

"You're being missed down at the party," I lie. "Theodore is asking around for the two of you."

"Please don't tell him you found us up here," Ramses bursts, his eyes as big as a child's caught doing something wrong.

I fold my big arms across my chest, blocking their way out, and intimidating him. Fuck, I thought I was above such petty strategies, but right now I'd do anything to make him look bad in front of Princess.

"It's okay, Ramses," she says. "You can tell Mr. Mayor the truth. He'll be on your side, even more than I ever was."

He glances from her to me, his cheeks on fire. He really seems to be still just a boy, even though he must be about Princess's age.

"But, but," he stutters. "I can't just tell him, just like that."

Princess places a hand on his shoulder. "Ramses, please. I didn't listen to you all those years ago, because what you said sounded so, so, fantastic. It was like a scenario from a fantasy movie. But then Mr. Mayor came to Darkwood Falls with a different story, one that made me remember yours. I realize I made a huge mistake by not believing you, and he—" She looks at me, and my heart jumps as her caramel eyes rest on my face. "He indirectly made me see that I was wrong."

The young man turns to me, too, inspecting me up and down. There's something innocent about him. If I hadn't seen the way he drools over Princess, I might have even liked him, even wanted to protect him.

"Have you seen fantastic things in your life, Mr. Mayor?"

I glance at Princess, not sure what to say. She nods with reassurance.

"Some."

He takes a step to me, as if wanting to inspect me closer.

"And if I were to tell you there are people who manage to make themselves into fantastic beings, would you believe me?"

I don't answer, my eyes shooting to Princess.

"What is he talking about?"

"Please, Mr. Mayor, just listen."

"Years ago," Ramses says. "I discovered something about my uncle's business, something that I found, well, let's say disturbing. I brought Princess here with the intention of telling her, and then showing her the file, but—" He bites his lower lip, cheeks reddening. "It sounded crazy. She thought I was trying to impress her with fantastic scenarios in order to get into her pants and...." He shakes his head.

"Never mind, it doesn't matter now. She called me up a few days ago, and said she now believed me, because she found some evidence of her own. But you can't tell my uncle you found us here, he can't be warned."

I close the door and lean with my back against it.

Princess swallows hard, obviously uncomfortable with the situation. She grabs one of the files and clutches it to her chest like a shield.

"I was wondering about Sullivan's acolytes putting a sex drug in my drink," she says. "I went through the minutes of Sullivan's meetings that I attended the past year, the e-mails I drafted for him, the people he had me call up. Going farther down memory lane, I remembered this talk I had with Ramses many years ago, before I even started working at City Hall. I remembered Ramses telling me about a man his uncle was doing business with, a man who owned a viper farm. It turns out it was a special kind of viper." She lifts an eyebrow, and it's all I need in order to understand. We're both thinking about the viper that slithered out of Spikes' mouth.

"Years ago," she continues, "when Ramses brought me here, he told me this viper farmer worked on ways to use their venom in order to strengthen humans. He showed me this file, and said what I'd find in it would change the way I viewed the world."

"After I left Darkwood Falls," Ramses takes over, now eager to share what he discovered like a mad scientist. "I kept track of the viper farmer and his work. Now his technology is so advanced it gets people, let's say, pregnant with these vipers, causing them to become some sort of serpent shifters in the process."

I lock eyes with Princess. So Spikes was *pregnant*. In a flash, I make all the necessary connections in my head—they needed the sex drug to get Princess desperate for sex, and impregnate her. I don't know why her of all people yet, but I will find out if it's the last thing I do.

The fur sprouts on my back, anger triggering a violent reaction. I won't be able to keep the wolf in check, and I'm afraid I'm going to shift right here, in front of Ramses.

I have to barge out and hurry down the stairs, taking two and then a whole flight at a time. I have to avoid the people on the ground floor, so I stalk through the dark on the first floor, throwing myself out through a window when I can't keep the wolf in check anymore.

My clothes fly off my body into shreds in Theodore's garden, and I can only hope no one finds them by the time I come back. I race through the woods, struggling to come to terms with this ache, need, and anger that inflate my chest. It's liberating, speeding through the woods in my wolf form, seeking exhaustion if not relief.

But when my head clears of the hotness my first thought is of Princess—I left her alone with Ramses. This is how a new torment begins. Flashes of her kissing him light up in my head, the young man sweeping the files off the desk and laying her on it, kissing her madly and working on his fly, ready to stick it in her.

I growl with such menace that the animals around seek shelter behind trees and bushes. Wolves and foxes, all cowering away from the raging beast that I've become. I head back to the manor, my snout sniffing for their scent, trying to single out the smell of arousal. And I find it.

His arousal. He wants her, oozing chemicals, sweating his desire for her. I track them to the gardens, and peek from behind a perfectly groomed bush to find them on a bench.

They're sitting angled to each other, the hem of her shiny red dress pooling on the ground. They're not holding hands, and she frowns, clearly focused on the information he seems to be giving her. But the young man's face is still flushed. He's nervous, and overflowing with desire for her. He makes a move to take her hands, and it's all I can do not to jump from the bushes and snap his throat between my jaws. I'm about to lose the battle with myself, but my brother Drago senses my predicament again.

"Ramses," he calls from the top of the stairs that lead to the back terrace of the manor. "Your uncle is looking for you. Let Princess enjoy the fresh air, you'll be right back."

Ramses looks from Drago to Princess, while I can feel my brother's eyes fixed on the bush where I'm hiding. He must have kept an eye on Princess since the moment she came back down without me, and now he's caught my scent in the bushes. He knows the poor boy has put himself in harm's way by getting close to Princess, and I can tell he's worried I might lose control. I myself am afraid it will come to bloodshed.

"I'll be right back," Ramses tells Princess, and makes to go. But on a second thought he returns and kisses her on the cheek. It's harmless, but she giggles, and I'm about to lose it.

Luckily for him he is out of sight when I stalk out of the bushes, my predator eyes on Princess.

Princess stiffens, gripping the edges of the bench when she sees me emerge, rustling the leaves and cracking twigs.

"Nero," she yelps.

"In the flesh," I say in the deep, dangerous voice of the wolf. My eyes glow with jealousy and frustration. She white knuckles the edge of the bench. Without the werewolf's calming effect on her senses, she gets to experience to the fullest what it's like to have the big bad wolf stalking you from the bushes.

"Why did you burst out of the attic like that?" She manages, but her voice trembles. "I had to find an explanation for that, I gave Ramses a load of crap."

"Ramses was focused on something else, I'm pretty sure he wasn't even listening to your explanations."

"He did tell me a lot more about the viper farmer. I'll come find you after I've talked this out with him."

"You can tell me now." I lay down on the ground on my paws, my big black body gleaming in the lights from the manor. She swallows hard.

"What is it?" I slur. "It's not like you see me in my beast form for the first time."

"What of Ramses? He can come back any moment."

I tighten my jaw so much that my teeth crunch. It makes Princess wince.

"Be honest with me, Princess. How do you feel about Ramses?"

"He's my childhood friend."

"Not your crush?"

She blushes. "It's him who used to be infatuated with me. I actually feel a little guilty for playing on those feelings now."

Ramses appears in the door to the terrace, talking to someone, but I can tell he's eager to get back here. He fidgets from one leg to the other as if he needs to pee. He's impatient to get back to Princess.

"Come on. Straddle me, and hold on tight."

"But—"

"Now, if you don't want the big bad wolf to eat your Ramses." I hiss his name through my teeth. I can't believe I actually threatened to harm an innocent man in order to make a woman do what I want her to. For the first time in centuries, I acted like a villain, and I'm not even sorry. Princess is mine. I can more or less accept that other men want her, but acting on that is a crime punishable by death.

Princess grabs her dress and walks over, looking like Cinderella hurrying away from the ball. She straddles me, grabbing the fur on my nape.

"Like this?" she whispers. Her body chemistry is running wild, I can smell it. She's nervous, but excited.

"Hold on tight."

I leap with her into the bushes, running through the gardens towards the woods, but not so fast to make her sick, or lose balance. I need her to easily keep herself on my back, but she stops me in only a few minutes.

"Please, I need to get down." She's sounds dizzy, sick. She unmounts, wobbly on her feet.

I stand up on my back legs, helping her over to a sort of podium with a slab of stone over two bulkier, vertical ones. It looks like an old stone altar, weeds in its corners and between the cracks. I narrow my wolf eyes, remembering something.

"An old serpent worship place in Lord Theodore's garden?"

"It's ancient, Theodore says it's been on his family's property for centuries," Princess explains, leaning on it. I grab her waist with my big furry hands, helping her up.

"God, you're huge," she whispers. In my wolf form and on my feet I'm even bigger than normal. I'm the tallest of my brothers, even if not the broadest.

"You should see Conan and Hercules. They're double my size."

"Are they black, too?"

"You like your werewolves black?"

"It's not what I meant."

Fuck, do I have to get jealous every time she mentions another man? I answer, even if only to prove to myself that I'm not a total dick.

"Conan is brown. Hercules is white. But I didn't bring you here to talk about my brothers. I came to talk about you. You can't expose yourself like that, flirting with men. It's clear Sullivan's acolytes were here to get you pregnant with a viper, I won't have you exposed to that."

"But Ramses is not an outsider. He is from Darkwood Falls." She lifts her chin and places her hands on her hips as if she's just been waiting to slap me over the snout with this.

"Yes, but he's been gone a long time. He could have been corrupted. Remember Spikes and the viper that slithered out of his mouth. I couldn't sense him the way I can sense serpents, so basically anyone can be an acolyte."

"Ramses would never."

"I thought I would never do what I'm doing right now." I sidle up to her, now very close, a towering big black wolf, my eyes blazing.

Color stains her cheeks, and my heart aches. I step back, giving her room, but it goes against everything I *really* want to do. Namely to lay her down on that slab, pushing her legs open and sticking my cock inside of her, making her mine.

"Nero, I'm tired of living in a prison," she pleads, sincerity in her voice. "I'm tired of pretending, of keeping up this façade. It's exhausting. Besides, I'm not even sure anymore that the werewolves' control over this town will mean freedom. It could be as bad as the serpents' control." She raises her beautiful white face to me, questions in her eyes.

"And what brought you to that conclusion?"

"The night I went to dinner with my dad and Theodore, they told me things about you. They told me about the headmaster and the teachers at the orphanage where you grew up. That they had been torn apart by beasts."

"They told you that, huh?"

"I didn't believe it at first, really. Some of the things Theodore said just didn't fit. You became of age centuries ago, not in the day of Wall Street, the time of finance and the Cayman Islands."

She waits for an answer, but I can't give it to her. Not the direct answer she wants, because I couldn't bear the contempt in her face. But I can't hide the truth from my mate, the nature of our bond won't allow it.

"I never denied that I have dark sides, Princess." As if on cue, the wind starts to rustle through the shrubbery, laden with bad omens. The bushes aren't so neatly groomed in this part of the gardens that are closer to the woods. I doubt the gardener has been here recently, the place seems wild, dark.

"Werewolves are, indeed, beasts, there's no point in pretending differently," I continue, keeping my tone even. "It's a truth we have to accept, as do all those we protect. Sometimes, in order to serve and protect, we have to do terrible things."

"You mean tearing those men apart was a necessity?"

Judging by her body chemistry, she wants me to convince her I'm not a villain. She wants to believe in me, and it's breaking my heart. "Please, Nero. Tell me the truth."

But it's not the truth that she really wants. She wants me to give her a sweet white lie, but I can't do that. I couldn't lie to my mate if I wanted to. I could avoid talking about certain things, but when she asks a direct question I'm helpless.

"I'm not a good person. I never claimed I was." I start pacing around her, in a circle around the altar. "What they told you was a version of the real story, Princess. In truth there was no Wall Street or Cayman Island, but trade in Venice, the Medici and corrupt cardinals."

"My God," she whispers. "You did kill those people."

"They weren't good people, Princess—not that it's an excuse. I committed murder, and I stand by my actions."

"Then how are you better than the serpents?"

"I don't know if we are, but we do want the best for the people of Darkwood Falls." I stop in front of her again. It's hard to take the tears in her eyes, the disappointment, but it's how things are. "The serpents have kept a grip on this town for a long time, keeping the females locked in, making sure they didn't get to mate with werewolves, because there was a high chance that later the hybrids would produce fated females. Which is what happened."

"And now you and your brothers are here to take over control because you feel this town and its women belong to you. But that's not better, Nero. We want freedom, we want to come and go as we please, live as we want, like everyone else."

"That's not possible for a very simple reason—if the serpents can't have you, as soon as you're unprotected they will kill you all."

"But if they wanted to kill us, couldn't they have done it from the start? Why take over this town, why keep it in their hands for so long, when they could have simply wiped it out?"

"This is where the elite comes in, people like your father."

"My dad?"

"My brothers went a little deeper with the research after we settled here because they asked themselves the same questions. Turns out that was the original plan of the serpents, killing the people of this town. After they wiped out the werewolves in the great massacre, including the elders and our parents, they came to do the same to Darkwood Falls. But by that time the town had developed a bit, and some of the women had sons that had made fortunes due to their unusual abilities—the hybrids weren't werewolves, because they hadn't been conceived by werewolves with fated females, but they did have unusual strength, speed, and some had supernatural abilities. They had made money, contacts, they had power, so they had something to offer the serpents. This is how an alliance came to be. Your father's ancestor was among the most powerful men in town."

Princess stares at me with an open mouth as she listens to the story.

"My God." Then, after she regains some of her composure, "Does that mean that my dad has supernatural abilities or something? Because I can't imagine—"

"No, the hybrids didn't mate with supernaturals, so their abilities got diluted over time. Only the females retained the gene of the

Fated Female from the original werewolves. That's something that doesn't go away, not even after thousands of years."

Princess ponders, looking all over my body as if she can understand the story better by doing that.

"Do you think I'm a fated female?" She whispers. She wrings her hands, anxious about the answer.

"Yes," I reply, as even and cold as I can.

"But not for you." It's not a question, which is the only reason why I can withhold the answer. My feelings for her storm inside of me, whirling in my chest. I want to grab her shoulders, look her in the eye and tell her that I imprinted on her, but that I have to let her go because making her mine would put her in as much danger as being out there for the serpents to grab.

She nods at my silence, disappointed. "I understand. Well, then, you won't mind if I tell you this—" She gives me a defying glare. "I am a sensual woman with a hot temperament. I didn't obey Sullivan back in his day, and went looking for fun with men, and I will continue to do that. If you don't want it to be Ramses or strangers, fine, but in that case I will accept one of the locals. There is someone in town who's been interested in me for a while now, and I intend to go out with him soon. Just so you know."

Every word is a blade through my heart, even though I'm aware she just wants to hurt me. It's working.

"You mean you'd accept a man you don't even like because you need sex, no matter how meaningless?"

"It won't be meaningless. I admit I'm not one of those women who can use a man for the pleasure alone, without sentiment." Then she gives me the final blow. "I intend to open my heart and fall in love with him."

Something snaps inside of me, and I grab her tightly.

"You are a fated female, and you have to be with a werewolf. One day one will imprint on you, and you'll have no choice but to give in to him." I know there can be no other werewolf because I already imprinted on her, and she's mine, but I'm angry and desperate. I would say and do anything to make sure she doesn't land in another man's arms.

"Sure, no problem. But I'm a twenty-seven year old woman, I need and want a man in my life. Until I meet my werewolf, I'm free."

I squeeze her small waist, barely keeping in check my need to crush her to me. "No man will ever touch you, or I swear to God I'll rip his head off. If you need a man, then I can fill in."

She looks up at me with thirsty eyes, drinking in the expression on my devil face, not scared, but like she's got me where she wanted me.

I want to tell it to her face that I can't fight this anymore, that I can't fight the passion, but I clench my teeth, keeping it in. I bend down to her, refraining from touching her lips yet. I start transforming back into a human, wanting to touch my human lips to hers, but then surprise. She puts her hands on the sides of my face, staring at me out of those caramel eyes as if she wants to imprint the moment in her heart.

"No, don't shift," she whispers. "I want to have you like this, as a beast."

But I look more like a devil than a wolf. I don't have a real snout, but my lips are dark and hard as concrete. Yet I am a beast, a scary one, and I can't believe a woman would want to have me like this.

I step back just to look at her. By God, she's a vision sitting there on the ancient stone altar, her shiny red dress showcasing her queenly body. She looks like an offering to some ancient god—the serpent god, I recognize the kind of altar, even though I haven't seen one like in many centuries.

God, how I love the fine muscles in her legs, the way that she moves. She lies slowly on her back on the stone slab, all the while keeping her burning eyes on me. She is my mate, and I'm pulled to her, ready to serve her, give her pleasure. I place a knee on the slab, her legs opening wide to make room for the second one.

She stretches her arms above her head, arching her body upward, offering herself to me.

"Fuck me, Nero," she pants, and my cock hardens so much that it aches. But I have to wonder. Does she feel this passion for me only because she feels the mate bond, or is she really into me? One way or the other, tonight I'll make her love me.

"Oh, I'll make you beg for it this time, Princess."

"I already aaaaa—" She arches her head back, her red hair spilling over the edge of the slab as I kiss the inside of her thigh, going straight for those sensitive spots.

Her eyes scrunch, her plump mouth opening wide as I tear her panties with my teeth and lick her right between her folds. The stroke of my tongue is that of a man hungry for her taste.

I grip her buttocks under her red dress with big wolf hands, my claws starting to emerge, but I keep them back. I lick her harder, with all the lust I feel, my cock ribbed, the head purple with need.

"Oh, please, Nero." Her plea is heartfelt, but not heartfelt enough. I come up to her chest, kissing her beautiful swan neck, taking in the flavor of her skin.

"God, how I love your scent, your taste," I drawl, searching for those sweet plump lips. She offers them to me, kissing me hotly, taking my head in her hands. I want to go down on her again, but she won't let me.

"Take me, right here, right now, Nero."

I wanted to make her beg more, but I can't control myself anymore. I drive my cock inside her slick pussy, my fur standing on end as she mewls with pleasure.

"Ah, go deep," she pleads, and I push in all the way, her pussy clenching around me greedily. "Fuck me like you own me."

"Oh, God." I pump Princess like there's no tomorrow, a devilish black beast with golden eyes claiming a princess on a stone in the garden.

I can feel she's close to cumming, her pussy pulsing hotly around me. And when her cream bursts, coating my cock, Princess lifts her head, her face hot and flushed, staring into my eyes like she can't believe it. She's holding tightly with her hands to the slab above her head, using it to push her hips up to meet me.

"I'll have you cum for me, Nero."

God, I'm helpless against those words, and the way she says them. I come undone, flexing to pull out, but she tightens her legs around me, not letting me. I watch her face full of pleasure as I spill my seed inside of her, right here on the serpent god's altar. I pull Princess into my arms as I morph back into a human, spent, my brain still afloat with the pleasure of release.

We lie entangled on the slab for a long time, a naked man with a dangerous obsession embracing his woman in red. My arms flex around her, raw strength and muscle against her delicate body. Fuck, this isn't good, what I feel inside. These mating feelings are something not even I, a very old Alpha, can deal with. How could I ever expect poor Drago to?

"Why did you do this, Princess? Why did you make me cum inside of you?" I whisper in her ear. Damn it, I'll never feel like I've possessed this woman enough. I want to merge with her to the last cell of my body.

"Out of spite," she breathes. I disentangle from her just enough to look into her face.

"Spite? Against me?" If she only knew that the idea of her giving me cubs is enough to make me hard again.

"No. Against the serpents. Against Sullivan. He wanted to plant a viper inside my body, to make me into a serpent shifter, didn't he? How about I slap him across the face and get pregnant with a werewolf. With the Alpha, no less. Even if you never imprinted on me. We'd have one of those hybrids with special abilities, wouldn't we?"

This is the point where I'm supposed to let go of her, take distance, talk sense into her, remind her this isn't where she and I are going. But the pleasure her words awaken in my heart won't let me. On the contrary, I pull her closer, warming her against my body as the wind and the night chill intensify.

"Having the alpha's children could mean great danger to you, Princess, and to them. The serpents would hunt you down, and they'd stop at nothing to get you."

I search her face for signs of fear or regret. There aren't any. She smiles at me.

"Don't worry. I can't actually get pregnant today, I'm not ovulating."

The clouds break, thunder ripping through the sky.

"Apparently the serpent god is angry," I say, looking up.

Princess laughs as the clouds break again, the first drop of rain landing on the tip of her nose. I can't hold back and kiss it, then the rest of the raindrops that follow, splashing on her face. Before she realizes what's happening I enter her again, enjoying the tight, slick inside of her body that I feel so entitled to. Soon I'm pumping her like an animal, my body sliding on hers, only her soaked red dress between us.

I take her vigorously, one hand on her back, steadying her, the other slipping under her bra. I cup her breast and groan as the perfectly round, white mount of flesh fills my palm.

"Tell me you love me, Princess," I plead in a guttural voice, burning with our connection.

She stares at me, her soaked red hair coating the stone.

"I—" But she doesn't finish, her body shifting up and down as I pump her. I drive my cock harder into her, my teeth clenching.

"Tell me," I demand. "Even if it's not true. Just say it."

There's menace in my eyes, I can feel it. My irises begin to glow, shining like flashlights on her face.

"I love you," she whispers, obeying my command. I close my eyes and lean my head back, going drunk with the sensation. I choose to believe her, at least for a moment, pouring myself into her.

When I look down at her again, riding high on my climax, I see the need and the silent request in her face—she wishes I'd say the same, she expects it, needs it. But the love declaration that threatens to leave my mouth isn't a simple 'I love you.' I want to grab her face and growl, 'I own you,' 'You'll have to kill me to get rid of me,' or 'I'll stalk you till the end of my days.'

So I keep it to myself. I descend from my climax and embrace her, protecting her from the downpour with my body until it stops. Our chests rise and fall into each other as we breathe in sync, her hands running lovingly along my back. I kiss her neck as the rain stops, and the wind carries Ramses' calls over from a short distance. He's calling her name, and he's not alone. People have started a search party for her through the storm.

"Quick," Princess reacts, pushing me off of her. "They're going to discover us."

She sounds downright desperate to keep what happened from the world. She grabs my hand, pulling me after her. I run naked through the garden, following her until we reach a darker side of the manor. She pushes a door open, but as soon as we've entered the dark, chilly corridor, I halt.

I grab her elbow, forcing her to turn around. "A friend, right? Is that really all that Ramses means to you? Or did you just say that to keep the beast tame?"

"Nero, what's gotten into you?"

"You were afraid of him finding us together. Why?"

"No, it wasn't that."

"Don't lie to me, Princess," I snap, jerking her arm. "He means more to you than you admit. You're worried that, if he finds out about us, he won't want you anymore, is that it?"

She looks at me shocked. "You can't be serious."

"Don't you dare start an affair with him behind my back, Princess. Or I swear to God I'll fucking kill him."

CHAPTER VI

Princess

Nero snatches a blanket for me from a dark, empty room, an old suit for him from one of Theodore's old wardrobes, and sneaks me out of the manor. He drives me home in silence, his jaw ticking, and in secret my heart blooms.

I can't help glancing at him often, even though what I really want to do is stare him full in the face, letting my eyes trace each one of those hard, masculine features. I faked the outrage at what he said to me about Ramses. In truth, I relished his jealousy like nothing before in my life, and I can't get enough of those feelings imprinted on his face.

Imprint.

I remember that one day he will imprint on a woman, and that woman won't be me. All that he feels for me is sexual attraction, and hey, I'm ecstatic about it, but if I came into question for him as his mate he would know it by now, wouldn't he?

I remember that sexy Latina Paola Valdez, the intimate way in which she talked to him and touched him, the look of familiar recognition in his face when he saw her. He walks me through the secret tunnel to my room and he wants to leave right after that, but I whip around, throwing the blanket he wrapped me in off my shoulders.

"What is it about Paola Valdez that earned her a long-term relationship with you?"

He blinks, confused. "Excuse me?"

I turn around like on a catwalk and prance naked to the wardrobe, feeling his eyes on me as I do it. I continue speaking as I sift through gowns on the rack.

"I hear you had a long-term relationship with her. You went to see her often, not always for sex. So you wanted more than that from her."

He pauses, which can only mean I'm actually onto something here, and I don't want it to be true. I want him to persuade me that he doesn't feel anything for her, that he never has. I want him to tell me I'm the only one he ever wanted.

"Paola was, indeed, something special."

The blood drains from my body, bitterness flooding my mouth. I keep my back at him, barely fighting the rage inside. "You imprinted on her, and somehow life separated you?"

He doesn't reply, but I can feel his eyes searing my back.

"You can tell me," I push. "I won't be jealous."

"Won't you?"

Damn it. I pick a gown, slide it down my body and turn around to face him with my back straight, my stare proud.

"If she is special to you, then why sleep with *me*, Nero? Why get my hopes up? Now let's be frank with each other. You know that I have feelings about you, why do you play with me like this?"

"You would have taken another lover if I hadn't done what I did tonight."

I snort angrily. "And when my own mate comes along? What happens then, huh? Will you tell him, hey, I fucked your fated mate, but it's over now that you came into the picture? If he'll feel about me like Drago feels about Arianna, you'll have a war on your hands. If you were a normal man, okay, he wouldn't feel hurt, because what do humans know, right? But you're a werewolf who knew I was a fated female. Which means you knew you were fucking some other guy's woman."

"I'm sorry," he says.

"Really? That's all you have to say?"

"What else would you like to hear?"

"Well, how about an explanation for your reaction back at the manor? Why threaten to kill Ramses?"

"I told you, he could be dangerous. He could be trying to impregnate you with a serpent, and for that process you don't need to be ovulating. The snake lives and grows inside of you, its cells soon merging with yours, and turning you into what Sullivan was. Is that what you want?"

I stare at this tall, athletic alpha with the impossibly handsome face and the golden eyes, wanting with all I have for him to fall in love with me. I walk to him, anger blazing in my face.

"Back in that garden, all I wanted was to avoid that people found us together. That would have messed things up for both of us. But then you went ballistic about Ramses out of nowhere. That just doesn't add up. And neither does your demanding that I tell you I love you while you fucked me."

"I don't want you to be alone with that Ramses guy until things clear up, that's all."

I keep staring at him, trying to assess his emotions.

"You confuse me, Nero. You're cold and reserved to me, but then destiny finds a way to get us in an intimate situation, and you're the most passionate and fabulous lover. Even more than that. You want to hear me say I love you, and you talk like a jealous lover when other men enter the game."

I walk to him, keeping my chin up. "I'm going to ask this one last time—is sexual attraction really all you feel for me?"

He towers over me like a god that's a misfit in this human world, especially like this, dressed in one of Theodore's old suits, the jacket open over his magnificent naked body. I have hope of seducing a love declaration out of him, and I slide my hands under the sides of his jacket, caressing those stone hard muscles.

"I'm going to admit one thing," I say lasciviously. "I called Ramses up because of what I remembered about the viper farmer, but also because part of me hoped his presence would make you jealous."

Nero grips my wrists, his jaw ticking. For a moment I think he's going to push me away, but what he does is push me towards the bed slowly as he speaks. It seems he's choosing his words carefully, his eyes burning like golden coals.

"I can't tell you exactly how I feel about you, Princess. But the sexual attraction is so fucking out of this world, that even the smallest touch lights me up. I never thought this was even possible between two people, and I'm fucking five hundred years old."

My body catches fire as Nero bends down and presses his carnal mouth to mine, his big hands caressing the gown off me. He's kissing me wildly, pressing my now naked body to him, and cupping my ass with both his hands like he's greedy for it. His tongue possesses my mouth, my breasts crushed against his concrete muscles, and cream trickles between my folds.

"Oh, how I want you, Princess," he whispers, his warm breath in my face.

"Nero, you incredible beast," I breathe, unable to control myself. I let my hands roam under the sides of his jacket, my palms splayed over his naked chest and downward. I lick my lips, watching what I'm doing as Nero tilts his head back with his eyes closed as if he's enjoying the most exquisite sensation. I use the chance to open his fly with one hand, while my other hand enjoys his body like he's candy.

I give in to my burning instincts and lick those muscles, going down to my knees. Nero grabs me under my armpits and tries to stop me, but it's too late. I take his iron hard cock in my mouth, sliding down to his balls and sucking with all I got. I only stop to tell him exactly what I feel.

"I love sucking you off, you have the cock of a god."

"Fuck, Princess." He grabs my hair and pushes it into my mouth so hard that he cums, his seed bursting down my throat, his cock throbbing. He groans, and I'm sure everybody in the house can hear it, but I don't give a damn. I squirm against my own thighs and cum as well, but that's the crazy effect Nero Wolf has on me.

He scoops me in his arms and carries me to the bed, all the while kissing me deeply. His mouth stays firmly on mine as he parts my legs and pushes his rock solid cock inside of me. My eyes snap wide, my mouth disengaging from his.

"My God, how is that even possible?" I shriek, but Nero's carnal mouth takes over mine again. He moans as he takes me like a master, pumping into me, my hands gliding down to cup his muscular butt, and drive him as deep as possible inside of me. I want to feel him flood every cell of my body.

If he can be so hard after I've just sucked him off, then he must be in lust with me, even if not in love, and that delights me. His huge cock slides over my sweet spot, building me up until I explode around him, my fingernails digging into his back under his suit jacket.

He drops exhausted by my side, wrapping his arms around me and inhaling the scent of my hair. I breathe in his masculine scent of wild forests, wanting to hold on to the moment forever. I want Nero

Wolf to belong to me, I want to sleep in his arms and breathe in his scent every night for the rest of my life.

"Nero," I whisper.

"Hm." The sound of his voice and the way he caresses my naked body tells me he feels the same, but it could be just wishful thinking.

"What does Paola Valdez mean to you? I need to know."

The caresses stop. "We used to sleep together. We're not anymore."

"Do you wish you were?"

"I wouldn't be in your bed right now if I did."

"Well, she sure wants to resume your affair."

"What Paola and I had is in the past, and that's where it's going to stay. And I think she knows that."

"You may be old and experienced Nero, but I see in regard to women you're naïve. I can assure you she'd fuck the daylights out of you, she was drooling after you tonight."

I feel his smile against my hair. "Naïve. Trust me, Princess, I'm anything but naïve."

I look up, resting my chin on his chest. "So you don't feel anything for her anymore? Lust, passion?"

He looks straight into my eyes as he says, "No," and I believe him. Even if only for a moment.

"Then send her away, Nero. I just.... She makes me uncomfortable. It's something about the way she looks at people, and the way she looks at you."

His face turns from relaxed, even a little high, to forbidding.

"I can't do that."

"Why not?"

"Please don't ask me that. I promise you that by the time this is over you'll know, but I can't let Paola leave Darkwood Falls just yet."

My cheeks light up. "This woman won't stop until she gets into your bed, Nero. If you and I are going to continue what we have, whatever you want to call it, I won't be just one of the women in your life. I will be The One, even if only for a little while, until my mate shows up." I pause, my lips puckering. "Or yours."

He brushes a red tendril behind my ear. "I can't get rid of her, Princess, not yet. I got her here for a reason, and I still need her."

I frown. "But it was Theodore who got her here, not you. And he did it in order to use her against you in some way."

Nero smiles, and I see the deeper wisdom behind the face of a young god. "I know."

I sit up, staring down at him, feeling dignified even though I'm naked. "You mean you steered this entire thing? Her arrival here?"

He brushes the side of my breast with his finger, and pulls me back into his arms. His cock is hard for me again, but as much as I desire him, I don't think I can make love to him again. I'm exhausted, and sore inside.

"Like I said, Princess, don't ask me questions that I can't answer just yet. Trust me for a little while."

"Trust you," I whisper, relaxing in his embrace against my better judgment.

Princess

WHEN I WAKE UP NERO is no longer here, of course. The high window is open, the curtains blowing in the pleasant breeze, and I can't repress a smile. I caress the place by my side where he slept, and I know he hasn't been gone long. The sheets are still warm.

I lie back down and put my cheek on his pillow, breathing in his scent and getting that cozy sensation I did last night, when I fell asleep in his arms.

I walk down the stairs to breakfast singing, my hand sweeping the banister. I know Nero isn't in love with me the way I am with him, so madly and inexplicably, but he's in lust, and he can't keep his hands off me. I'll take it for now, and I'm going to enjoy it while it lasts, making the best of it.

But I stop in my tracks when I see Dad at the breakfast table in his wheelchair, glowering at me like he wants to ground my ass for the rest of my life.

I head to the table, stiff as I take my usual seat across from him. The butler comes with more sausages and boiled eggs, placing them on the table and then lingering with his hands behind his back. But Dad waves him away. When he leaves, the man looks at me like he caught me on the wrong foot, too.

"One of the mayor's people offered to take me home last night." Dad cuts a sausage with his fork like he wants to kill it, and pops it into his mouth. "While getting ready for bed, thinking you weren't here, I heard a man's groans of pleasure echoing through the halls. It was faint, but I know what I heard. Now I can't help but wonder—were you here with the mayor last night, Princess?"

My throat constricts, and I have trouble swallowing the food in my throat.

"I didn't know you were home." I sound like somebody is strangling me.

"Was it the mayor?"

Hell, I can't lie to him. I look down at my plate. "Yes."

His fork clatters on the table. "Damn it, Princess. I told you Nero Wolf was a dangerous man. He is a beast! How could you give yourself to him?" He coughs, clutching the napkin and taking it to his mouth.

I lean over the table, reaching out to take his hand but he leans away.

"Dad, before Nero came to this town you were afraid that Sullivan might try to hurt you. You were afraid he might even try to murder you, since he doesn't need you to finance his campaigns anymore. Nero and his people can free you of his terror once and for all, believe me. You and everybody else who fear Sullivan."

"Free us?" He coughs again in his napkin, but he's determined to continue. "Nero Wolf and his lot aren't any better than Sullivan and his people. You heard what he did to the headmaster and the teachers from the orphanage where he grew up. When he's done with us, he's going to murder us all."

"You don't know what it was like for Nero and his brothers at the orphanage, Dad, what those people did to them."

"Oh, and you do? How, because he told you, right? And you just believed him."

"He wasn't lying, Dad, I know that for a fact."

"Jesus Christ, how could you sleep with him, Princess, knowing what he's capable of? He used wolves on those people, hell hounds for all we know! That bestiality could turn against you, my daughter, anytime!"

I inhale deeply, keeping the ton of things I want to say on the tip of my tongue. There's no point arguing with him on this one, I have to put this differently.

"He sure won't leave Darkwood Falls with half of the elite's money, because he's got much more than he needs. And he isn't the puppet of shady organizations, like Sullivan."

"No matter what, you shouldn't trust Nero Wolf."

"Dad, whatever you're afraid of, Nero can help."

"Help? Jesus, Princess, you're so naïve. Even if that were so, we'd be confined to this town for the rest of our lives, because otherwise Sullivan and his people would kill every man or woman of Darkwood Falls as soon as they step into another town. And while it wouldn't be so bad for me, because I'm an old man and a cripple, it would be a death sentence for you, my daughter. And for your mother who, as you can see, spends months out there, on the pretense that she's attending social events and fashion shows."

"Pretense?"

"Oh come on, Princess, don't tell me you never imagined she was sleeping with other men." I want to say something, but he stops me. "Not that I blame her. I haven't been able to deliver in a long time, and she's no longer young or stupid enough to get pregnant or catch a disease if she has sex with other men. But I love her, believe me, more than my own life. She gave me many marvelous years, and she gave me you. I won't have her exposed to Sullivan and his goons out there. Sullivan wants Nero Wolf gone from this town at all costs, and I will help him. After that, you'll all be free."

"No, Dad, we won't be. It'll be the other way around. If we don't let Nero and his wolves help us, Sullivan and those backing him up will retake the town, and wipe it out, *after* they take over everybody's money and power. They won't risk being overthrown again."

Dad frowns, the skin on his old face creasing. "Nero's wolves? What do you mean?"

So Dad doesn't know about werewolves and serpent shifters. And it's not like I can enlighten him about it, no matter how much I want to. He's old and ill, such things would either give him a heart attack, or shake his trust in me so badly that I might never be able to save it.

"I mean his people. I said wolves because of his last name."

I push my chair back and hurry to Dad's side, sitting down. I look him straight in the face.

"Dad, I'm sorry I have to tell you this, but it's necessary—I'm in love with Nero. I don't know if he feels the same, but I know he would never hurt me, and I trust him. Please, for my sake, just give him a chance."

Dad shakes his head. "My sweet girl, I understand your fascination with him. He is a magnificent beast of a man, and his attention can be addictive, but don't fool yourself. Men like Nero Wolf don't fall in love. They use women, drain them of connections, influence and money, then they toss them away like used rags. I won't watch that beast do with my daughter what he did with Paola Valdez."

"What did he do with Paola?"

"He destroyed her soul."

"And how do you know that?" I fold my arms across my chest. "Don't tell me she made confessions to you."

"Actually she did. After you and him disappeared from the party last night Paola came to me, seeking consolation. She was a scorned woman, and I was the father of her rival, so she felt a strange connection. I did, too, to be honest. We were both hurting."

"You were hurting because of her," I say between my teeth. 'You wouldn't have even known I was with Nero if she hadn't told you, because I left the party with Ramses. If she knew about Nero and me, it's because she followed us, and then she came straight to you with a strategy."

"That may be true, but it doesn't change the fact that you did give yourself to Nero Wolf last night."

I press my lips together. There's nothing I can say about that.

"We talked a lot, Paola and I. Actually she drank booze and talked, I listened. She told me she had accepted Theodore's invitation because she'd been hoping to rekindle things with Nero, but apparently he was still a player and a hunter. She told me he was a hustler who makes women feel terribly desired until he gets what he wants from them—support for his business or lobbying ambitions, money for new ventures he doesn't want to risk his own for or, like now in your case, support against his enemies, people who stand in his way. He's very ambitious, shrewd and deadly. He's incredibly handsome, and he knows it, using it to manipulate women, then break their hearts like he did with Paola." He touches my chin gently. "And you, my daughter, will be next."

Could this be true? Has Nero given other women the same passionate love he's given me? Doubt darkens my mind. Could it be that Nero is only using me, even if only for sexual pleasure until he gets enough of me?

Nero

PAOLA PUSHES THE DOORS to my office open, prancing inside, one stilettoed foot in front of the other. Princess runs behind her.

"Hey, you can't just barge in there."

"Get out." Paola barks over her shoulder.

Princess's eyes shoot at me for yay or nay, and I nod. "It's all right."

Princess doesn't like it, I can tell. She's been aloof all day, getting out of my path every time I tried to approach. Watching her in her red office dress got me hot like a teenager with a permanent boner, and I wanted to take her right here on my desk, but she avoided me.

"Fuck you, Nero!" Paola bursts, slapping her hands on my desk. "You didn't have Theodore invite me to Darkwood Falls because you missed me, but because you wanted to use me against Sullivan. Had you fucked me, you would have done it thinking of your secretary."

"Keep your voice down." I walk around the desk to where Paola stands. "I don't want Princess getting that idea."

"You mean you don't want her to know that you're stalking her. Yes, I noticed the way you stared at her last night. You wanted to throw her on her back and bury your face in her pussy."

My cock twitches at those words. I stop an inch from Paola, looking down into her furious eyes.

"Princess wants me and only me in this world, while you would have made do with any one of my brothers."

"Oh, is that the reason why you refused to fall in love with me? Because I love to fuck?"

"Because you're not capable of deep feelings."

"Oh, and that red-headed brat who looks like Tinkerbell is? You've known her only a few weeks, you think you already know what's inside her heart?"

I glower at her, maddened by her attack against Princess. I'd never hurt a woman, but the more I look at this one the more I despise her. I bend my face down to her, fierce. I'm burning to tell her that I love Princess, that I imprinted on her, but if she's in with the serpents like I always suspected, that would be a death sentence for Princess.

"I've never been in love with you or anybody, and I'm not in love with Princess now. I fucked her, I admit it, and it was good, real good. I'd bend her over my desk and bang her again, that's true as well. But it's not like I'd do that with her any more than I'd do it with you."

My words are meant at pushing her away, angering her because I'd bang her or any other woman just the same, but they achieve the opposite. She calms down and gives me a hooded gaze, sex in her eyes. What I said actually turned her on.

"Then why don't you do it?" She reaches for the hem of her impeccable white blouse and lifts it over her head, now standing in front of me only in her bra.

"Paola, what are you doing?"

"Come on. Bend me over your desk and fuck me. You know how much I love a big dick in my ass. Imagine you're driving that python of a cock inside Tinkerbell while you do it, I don't care."

She unzips her pencil skirt while she talks, pushing it down. She turns around and bends over the desk, giving me a provocative look over her shoulder and reaching behind to grab my cock. It's slack. Like I expected, imprinting on Princess rendered me useless for other women. The only one my cock will ever stand at attention for is Princess, the need for her taking over my heart like a fucking disease, like an obsession.

There are no words to describe the disappointment on Paola's face.

"What is it, Nero? Am I not sexy enough for you anymore?" She knits her dark eyebrows. "Do me a favor, old lover—think of Princess Skye with her legs open right here, on your desk."

My cock twitches in her hand, lengthening and hardening. Fuck, the slightest thought of Princess is enough to make me horny. Rage and ambition transform Paola's face. She lets go of my cock and pushes her hand between her legs, starting to work on herself, releasing a loud moan.

"What the hell are you doing?" I hiss through my teeth, but it's too late. Princess comes in, baited by her fake moans, and sees me standing by the side of a naked woman working her pussy on my desk.

"God damnit, Princess, this isn't what it looks like," I call, the look on Princess's face tearing my heart like a merciless claw.

She lingers there for a few moments, neither of us knowing what to do or how to react. I reach out and take a few steps towards her, but she bursts into tears, whips around and runs out, slamming the door behind her.

"Princess, no!"

Too late. She will never trust me again after what she saw, and there's nothing I can say or do to make this right. The world comes tumbling down on me.

"If she's got at least a trace of dignity she'll never let you touch her again," Paola says behind me, sick satisfaction in her voice.

Rage boils inside of me. This woman just destroyed all my chances of getting at least scraps of Princess's attention. Scenarios run wild in my head, of Princess running right into Ramses' arms, or maybe the arms of that local she told me about and that she was considering going out with.

"Oh, don't worry," Paola mocks, getting off the desk and starting to put her clothes back on. She achieved just what she wanted. "A woman like your Tinkerbell, beautiful, extravagant, she can get any man she wants. She won't be alone or neglected. She doesn't need you, and you know what—you don't need her either."

I want to turn around, grab Paola's arm and throw her out, but that would only destroy my plans. I need her, the entire pack does, the whole town.

I square my shoulders and turn around, staring coldly down at her.

"Do me one last favor, Nero. Tell me the truth. What do you feel for Princess?"

"Lust. I am in lust with her."

"More than you ever were with me, is that it?" There's bitter reproach in her words.

"Yes, but I've been with you longer than I've been with her."

She stares up at me in defiance. "You're so full of shit, Nero. But you don't fool me. You're crazy about this woman in a way you've never been about anyone in your life. You got me here because you wanted to use me, but guess what—I saw right through your plot." Her dark eyes seethe with wickedness and revenge. "You fooled me the first time, when you had me clinging to you, hoping there could be more between us than just an affair. After a while you didn't even sleep with me anymore, and I still did your bidding like a dog or, admittedly, like a horny bitch. But not this time, Nero. This time I knew what you were up to and I came prepared."

She sticks out her chin as she gives me the last blow. "You'll pay for what you did to me, and for wanting to do the same this time around. Neither you or your brothers will get out of this town alive, and you know what? Sullivan or the big boss, The Reaper, don't even have to show up in person. Their plans are far greater than what you can foresee, despite all of your experience and power. Sullivan has got someone in this town who will bring you down, and you don't even suspect who it is and how exactly they're going to do it. But know that I will be there to watch your downfall, and that it was the way you treated me that brought this upon you."

She stares into my eyes for a few moments, waiting for signs of worry or fear, but I'm too old and I've gotten too good at controlling the expressions of my face.

"By the time this is over, you will break, Nero Wolf. Make no mistake about it." She sidesteps me, walking to the door.

Princess

TEARS ARE STREAMING down my face as I knock on Arianna's door. The housekeeper opens it, her neutral face filling with worry the moment she sees me.

"Tell her I'm here, please," I manage among hiccups.

The housekeeper hurries up the stairs of the cozy Victorian house that is now adorned with colorful baby things. This is a nest of love and happiness, like what I would have loved to have with Nero as well. I cry harder as I realize once again that it's never going to happen.

I plop onto the coach until the housekeeper helps the heavily pregnant Arianna down the stairs. I shoot up to my feet.

"I would have come to you," I say, sniffling and wiping my nose. "I thought Beth would only let you know I was here, not help you down."

"I had to get out of bed, I can't bear to lie down anymore. Jesus, Princes, what's wrong?"

I put my arms around her and rest my forehead on her shoulder, shaking with sobs. She caresses my hair and sits down with me, holding me until I can speak again.

"I caught him with his ex, Arianna," I manage among sobs. "He was banging her on his desk, on the very desk he wanted to fuck me on earlier today. Dad was right, he's a playboy, a hustler, a heartbreaker. Damn, this hurts so bad."

Arianna looks at me with bewildered powder blue eyes. "Start from the beginning, love."

I do. I cry and sniffle in the napkins, feeling better with every word as I release it all to my best friend. She calls Janine, whose sports car screeches to a halt into the driveway in less than half an hour.

She drops her designer bag in a corner and hurries over in her business suit and pumps, her blonde bob shining in the light.

"I do believe that Nero Wolf has deep feelings for you," she says after Arianna and I fill her in. Our teacups lie empty on the table, and the housekeeper refills them.

"He didn't imprint on me, Janine, that much is certain. And if he didn't imprint on me, then he isn't in love."

"But he came here often to talk to Drago, and I think it was about you," Arianna puts in. "Nero looked like a dumped lover when he left here in the morning. Crazy hair, stubble, wild eyes as if he was clinging to some hope."

"Yes, he looked pretty down when he came back to the hotel at night," Janine chimes in.

"Do you get to see him often?" I whisper.

"He's been staying at my hotel ever since he came to Darkwood Falls, so we do run into each other a lot. He actually gave me a job to do."

"A job?"

"Investigation," Janine says. "Nero found out about my skills from Drago, and he told me about the serpent acolytes putting a sex drug in your drink. I activated my antennas, and it turns out that some of those guys had worked for Theodore Firtz until a few months ago."

I look into Janine's intelligent cobalt eyes. "Does that mean—?"

"That they may have been acting on his command. But that was only a suspicion at first. Not enough even for the werewolves to do anything about Theodore, but it's the reason Nero has been sniffing around Lord Fritz."

"Drago says his alpha brother always has had a life motto," Arianna chimes in. "Keep your friends close and your enemies even closer."

"That's why he's been doing Theodore favors," I whisper.

"Anyways, after I gave him this information about one of the serpents acolytes having worked for Theodore he thanked me, and said that would be all," Janine says. "But I couldn't stop." She heads to her bag, searching inside it.

Of course she wouldn't stop. Janine is a highly intelligent lady, a business woman by trade, and a detective by hobby. That's how she got Drago as a male escort for Arianna less than a year ago, without any of the town people getting the slightest whiff. In the end, it was her who discovered the werewolves, and it was due to her detective skills, which is something Nero saw and exploited.

She comes back with her tablet, turns it on, and shows Arianna and me files and information she discovered. It's reports about missing persons from the towns around Darkwood Falls.

"The acolytes that Nero took into custody were from these towns," she says. "So was Spikes, and I thought maybe he had family or friends who would miss him. Turns out he had been reported missing—even if only briefly."

"What do you mean only briefly?" I'm bursting with curiosity.

Janine swipes her long fingers over the tablet and shows us the file she hacked into from the police department of said town. The person who reported him—Lord Theodore Fritz.

"You gotta be shitting me," I react.

"Only a few days later Theodore withdrew his report—probably when he realized that Spikes fell into the hands of the 'enemy', so to say, and he didn't want the police digging *too* deep."

"Could it be that Theodore knew what these people were? That they had snakes inside of them?" Arianna says.

I get up to my feet, pacing the room, putting two and two together.

"It makes sense. It makes *perfect* sense." I turn to the girls, excited that we're getting to the bottom of this. "Theodore has been doing business with a viper farmer for many years. They were breeding those vipers in a special way. It was a viper that killed Spikes from the inside, and slithered out of him. And Theodore knew Spikes. It doesn't get any clearer than that, does it?"

"Yes, but what about the sex drug?" Arianna says, touching her swollen stomach, her face scrunched as if she's having contractions.

'Everything okay?" I inquire. She nods, eager to continue this conversation, but I'm not so sure.

"Problem is," Janine says, focused, "that the werewolves can sense serpents, but not acolytes. Not people who have snakes inside of them the way this Spikes guy did. So anyone could be an acolyte."

"And there are two types of acolytes, Drago told me," Arianna manages, hands splayed over her stomach. "Type A, people 'pregnant' with the snake, who will turn into serpents themselves, and type B, people who are simply serpents' puppets. Like Spikes. The snake is like a remote control. They all get inoculated in the same way, and it's a gamble, really, who becomes a serpent shifter and who remains a servant. Some get lucky, some don't."

"But then the question remains—what about the sex drug?" Janine ponders. "What does that have to do with you, Princess, and why did Spikes put that drug in your drink?"

"That drug would have killed me if I didn't have sex. So he wanted to bring me in a state where I wouldn't say no to anyone. Even if I would have been normally repulsed by that person."

"Then let's use the simplest logic," Arianna says. "Who is crazy about sleeping with you, but knows you'd never accept them under normal circumstances?"

One name comes to mind. "Theodore."

Arianna cringes, throwing her head back. I can see with the naked eye how her stomach constricts. Both Janine and I snap to her, the housekeeper Beth emerging from the back of the house, wild with worry.

"Quickly," Janine says, helping Arianna. "Call an ambulance. She's having her babies. I'll call Drago."

I stay with Arianna as the two women make the calls. She grabs my hand over her belly.

"Princess, don't you dare go confront Theodore about this."

I smile, but it's only to reassure her, because I won't let this go.

She and Janine would have me go to Nero with this. But! Theodore surely has protection in place against Nero and the werewolves, not to mention that he could have serpents ready to intervene for him. I can't imagine he stayed in Darkwood Falls as Sullivan's invisible hand unprotected, at the mercy of the werewolves in case all of this comes to light, like it just did.

No. But he sure won't see a reason to protect himself against me. On the contrary. Me he wants. I can get him to share his secret, make him think I'm on his side, even that I'm interested in him. I'll get Theodore to tell me where Sullivan hides, and the werewolves can take it from there.

The door bursts open, and Drago barges in.

"Damn, you were quicker than the ambulance," Janine squeaks.

Without a word Drago scoops Arianna up from the couch like she's a feather, planting a strong kiss on her plump lips.

"No ambulance will be quicker than me."

"Your friend at the obstetrics is ready, milady," the housekeeper throws in.

Janine grabs Arianna's hospital bag from the housekeeper, thanks the woman, and we follow Drago out of the house. We both get into Janine's sports car, and race behind Drago to the hospital.

CHAPTER VII

Princess

Two healthy chubby babies, beautiful as angels. I got to hold them both after Drago and Janine did, but then Nero came to the hospital, and I had to get out of here before we came face to face.

But as I leave the hospital something else floods my mind more than him, which is a first since the first night we spent together—how can I feel so much love for those two babies? I could cry with love and tenderness. I always expected I'd love Arianna's and Janine's children, they are like sisters to me, but like this, as if they were my own blood? It overwhelms me.

I heard that werewolves have this kind of affection for babies of their pack, and I'm pretty sure this is what Nero feels for his niece and nephew as well. But why does it feel the same for me?

Whatever the answer, these two babies give me more reason and strength to fight. I won't let them grow up in a town in which anyone could be a serpent acolyte, and I will do everything in my power to protect them.

Getting a date with Lord Theodore Fritz tonight is like running a blade through butter. He's ecstatic that I want to talk to him at his place. I tell him in a honey voice on the phone that I'd like us to be alone, except maybe for a valet that would tend to us.

I know how to make men break and give me what I want. I hate doing it, but the fate of Darkwood Falls is in my hands.

The moment the big black gates open to let in the limo Theodore sent for me, my heart constricts. Damn, I hate this. I can barely keep the smile on my face as I step out of the car, dressed in a leather corset and leather pants, patent leather stilettos on my feet.

Theodore opens his arms when he sees me, looking me up and down like I'm all made of gold.

"My God, Princess, you're so beautiful," he says, taking my hand and walking me inside the dining room that he's had prepared for a romantic evening.

'Wow, Theodore, I'm overwhelmed," I purr, touching the roses on the table and looking around.

"All for the most enchanting woman in the world," he says with a sleazy grin, stroking the back of my hand with his thumb. "I can't begin to tell you how happy and honored I am." He looks like he'd throw himself at me and kiss me, plunging his tongue inside my mouth if I gave him the slightest hint that I was willing, and my stomach twists.

But I manage a smile, heading toward my seat that Theodore pulls for me. "I must say, I was surprised when you called. Now that I see you dressed as Catwoman, I'm stunned."

"You don't approve?" I bat my lashes at him like a kitten.

"Oh, by all means, I love it. But I wonder." He takes a seat by my side, at the head of the table, angled to me in an intimate way. "Why take that kind of trouble for me?"

I give him the answer I have prepared while the valet pours red wine in a crystal glass. "I had a talk with the mayor on the night of the soiree. He reminded me that I can't see anyone who's not a local of Darkwood Falls, and that in this sense he isn't doing things any differently than Sullivan. He opened the subject because he saw me with Ramses, and he said Ramses wasn't 'local' enough, so to say, because he's been living outside of Darkwood Falls for so long."

"Princess, are you telling me you're thinking about a relationship? With me?"

I bite my lip as if I'm shy, but I continue. "Listen. Theodore, I know this is sudden, and it comes out of nowhere, but let's be honest with each other. We've known one another for decades, you've known me since I was a child. The more I grew into a woman, the more I felt your eye on me, and I know you find me, well, to your liking. I was wary of showing my own interest in you because, to be quite frank, I thought that one day I would marry outside of this town and leave forever. But since that's not going to happen anytime soon, I thought maybe, you would be the perfect choice."

"For a husband? Princess, are you proposing to me?" He stares at me with wide eyes. I can tell he groomed himself carefully before this date, his usually crumpled face nicely creamed, his hair combed back, his suit impeccable, his manicure fresh.

I look at him like I'm about to let go and be completely honest, as if I've been holding this inside for far too long. "Look, I'm already twenty-seven, and I'm not getting any younger. On the other hand, my father would never accept me being with some poor chump without a big family name and serious money. You and me, I think we go well together like that, don't we? We're both rich, we're both from Darkwood Falls, and we both need a partner. Or don't you need someone? Do you prefer to remain alone until the end of your days?"

There's skepticism all over his face, but he smiles and touches my hand.

"Let us eat, enjoy this evening."

And we do, but I eventually manage to steer the discussion in the direction that I want. A few hours later Theodore and I head outside to the back terrace with our glasses of wine to enjoy the gardens in the moonlight. He invites me to sit on the stone edge of the terrace, his eyes slipping down my body wrapped in leather.

The way I look in this outfit makes him hot, which is what permits me to be so direct about a relationship. I'm well aware men like Theodore, former playboys who led decadent lives until they were too spent to keep it up, usually back down when a woman comes with talk like this. But he's wanted me for a long time, and as long as he doesn't get me in his bed, thus ending the tension, my advances will only turn him on.

He winds an arm around my shoulders, and I feel the moment has come.

"I've been wondering," I start in a low, intimate voice. "Have you heard from Sullivan again after, you know…"

"Why would I of all people hear from him?" His face is close to mine, his breath on my cheek, and I know he's looking for a way to kiss me. I fight my disgust, and try to relax in his arms, but every cell of my body rebels.

"You were close, you and Sullivan. He told you secrets. You were the first to know about his affair with Christie, weren't you?"

"Yes, and I also knew he loved Arianna, even years after they broke up."

I nod, looking down at his hand as it makes its way over mine on my thigh. "Can I tell you a secret?" I purr.

"Anything."

"I always thought Arianna should have gotten back together with Sullivan."

"Really? You don't like her Wolf? I thought it was you and Janine Kovesi who introduced her to him."

"Yes, but here's another secret—we thought she'd just have her fun, and then dump him. We never thought she'd fall for him, we were certain she wanted someone of substance for a long-term relationship."

"Speaking of affairs and relationships that one takes seriously." He bends for the bottle of wine at his feet. "It's not easy for me to mention this, because of etiquette and all, but since we're sharing secrets—Wagging tongues say you're having an affair with the mayor. Is it true?" The suspicion in his tone cuts.

"And whose tongue has been wagging with that rumor? No, let me guess—Paola Valdez's. I'll have you know that she's the one sleeping with Nero. I caught them myself yesterday."

Theodore grins, as if he's got me exactly where he wanted me. "Is that why he acted like a mad beast today, during his meeting with the Council? Because you caught him with another woman?"

I swear the sky has just come crashing down on me. "Say what?"

"He hadn't shaved, his hair was messy, and his eyes bloodshot as if he'd been drinking since morning."

I swallow, my voice cracking. "I'm sure he's just worried I might go around telling people about him and Paola. Like I said, I caught them fucking on his desk." But I'm afraid my face betrays the truth.

"That's a good theory, and I'd even fall for it. If your father hadn't called me, awfully distressed, telling me his daughter has fallen in love with the mayor."

The world starts to spin with me.

"Then there's Ramses," Theodore says, sipping his wine like a gentleman, but I can sense the fury rising in him. "Who told me that Nero got in his way when he tried to get close to you. And that he suspects the mayor has an obsession with you." His eyes pierce mine.

I stutter with the glass of wine in my hand, not knowing what to say. I feel stupid, sitting here with this man, thinking I had him in the palm of my hand, when in truth he was only leading me on to expose me like this.

I place the glass of wine on the stone edge, feeling mortified, naked. This went terribly wrong, and I'm sorry I came here. I should have listened to Janine, and left this in the hands of the werewolves, helping them only with my counsel, not by taking action.

"I should probably leave now."

But Theodore grabs my hand. "There's no leaving now, Princess. You came here to use me, milk me for information and, were I just a little more stupid than I am, I would have fallen for it." His face changes with every word, turning mean, spiteful. "You wanted to play with my heart the way the mayor played with Paola's. But you're not as powerful as he is, Princess. He's a werewolf, he attracts women like a magnet and they are helpless against his charms. But you. You're just a pretty pussy, the likes of which I fucked dozens. There's nothing special about you, you're not good enough to make me lose my head."

His words feel like slaps on my face, but not because of what he says about me. "You know about werewolves?"

His face warps with an ugly grin. As if on cue, the bushes start to rustle, and all the muscles in my body flex as my brain puts me in the fight or flight mode. And when men with ghost-like pale faces begin emerging from the bushes, I'm sure I'll have a heart attack.

I retreat towards the manor as they advance, Theodore standing in place, watching the fear in my face as they start to shift. Their skin cracks, shredding and revealing slimy tissue underneath. Their human appearance shreds along with their clothes, humanoid worms rolling out from that cracking shell, transforming into human-sized serpents, forked tongues flicking out of their mouths.

I scream and cover my face, making myself small by the manor wall, certain this is it.

It's true what they say. Your life runs before your eyes like a movie when you think you're about to die. This is the first time I've seen serpent shifters with my own eyes, but I've heard enough about them to know that, when they make an entrance, it's because they're set on a kill.

But just as I hear one of them hissing really close, a metallic sound whips through the air, and slime hits the back of my hand. Somewhere in my head I know one of the serpents has been killed, but it's not enough to make me look up, not until a strong hand grips my wrist.

My eyes meet Nero's, his golden irises alight with focus.

"Get out of here, fast," he says, but then a female voice resounds behind him.

"And where do you suppose she can go, Nero?" It's Paola Valdez, joining Theodore. Has she been in the gardens all along? Have she and Theodore planned this whole thing? "This manor is full of serpents, she'll only land in their hands."

Nero shields me behind him, a leather jacket stretching over his broad back.

"What is it, Nero, love?" Paola mocks, but I can hear the hurt in her voice. "You wonder how the serpents got into this town despite your wolves' all-around surveillance?"

I grip Nero's leather jacket, keeping my body plastered to his, my breasts pushing into his back, but I peer around his side.

Paola Valdez, dressed in a black outfit like some kind of mobster queen, prances on her high heels toward us, while Theodore watches from under his unruly eyebrows.

"Well, you missed one very important detail—serpents are creatures of the earth. They dig holes and tunnels in the ground, this is how they emerged directly into the basement of this manor. You never thought about checking the underground, have you."

Nero doesn't reply, and I don't note a change in his body either. His big muscles are flexed, ready to fight, which shows he's sharply focused. But by now I know he's so skilled at hiding his emotions that he could be terrified out of his skin, and no one could tell.

She wants to say more, but Theodore steps in, looking like he can't wait to show me how wrong I was about him.

"You thought me so stupid to believe you'd want me, Princess? An extravagant beauty like you, wanting an old fuck? How stupid must a man be to believe the show you put up?"

"Look at them, the lover birds," Paola says full of bitterness, watching Nero and me. "He protects her with his own body, because he would be nothing without her. He imprinted on her, and he was desperate to keep it a secret in order to keep her safe."

My heart jumps, and my eyes shoot up at Nero. Is this true?

"And she looks at him like he's a god, wanting him with all she's got," Paola continues, full of resentment. "Let me tell you something

Princess, now that you're about to die, along with your lover—I came on to him the other day, but his cock was slack like a rag in my hand. Only when I prompted him to think of you did his body react, and you know why? Because you're his mate. He's deeply in love with you, Princess, you can die knowing that. The moment I realized that I put my hand between my own legs, and moaned to get you to barge in and catch us, make you think you were just one of his many conquests. But die knowing he wouldn't be able to fuck another if he wanted to. To him, you're the only woman in this world with a pussy."

Pieces of the puzzle come together in my head, the last one being the unbeatable proof he imprinted on me—the feelings I have for Arianna's children. As a werewolf's fated mate, I became part of the family, part of the pack, and I feel the family ties in my flesh. This is the best explanation for the way I feel about those two baby angels.

'What about the sex drug?" Nero asks, his voice deep, masculine and even, as if nothing out of the ordinary is happening here. "Did you have Spikes put it in her drink, Theodore? If, like you said, you fucked dozens like her in your life and she's nothing special, why go to such lengths to get her in your bed?"

Theodore's face draws. Explain that, sleazy bastard.

"Yes, Theodore, why?" I even manage a provocative smile.

"Oh, don't feel too good about yourself just yet," he spits. Something slithers under the skin of his neck, and I grip tighter to Nero's jacket. "It was Sullivan's idea, and you have to admit it was brilliant. What better way to lead the werewolves to extinction than to corrupt their fated females? Fuck them and maybe even get them pregnant with serpent babies. And I wouldn't have fucked you alone, Princess." He enjoys saying this, I can tell. "It would have been a gang bang and, with a little luck, you would have gotten pregnant."

My stomach constricts, and I want to puke, but I don't get to. Nero shifts, springing out of his clothes, his fur sprouting and his body enlarging into the big black beast that looks like a devil, making all the serpents around him shrink back. Even Paola looks up at him like she's just seen a nuke. She takes a step back and stumbles, falls, and hits her head against the stone edge where I sat with Theodore before.

As for Theodore, he gawks at Nero with a mix of fear and admiration. He surely didn't expect the alpha werewolf to be so big, blocking out the light from the high terrace window behind us.

"I'll be damned," he whispers, but then his face disappears inside a big black ball with deadly sharp fangs.

The next thing I know Theodore's body sways before my eyes, wriggling from between the beast's fangs until it drops on its knees right in front of me. Blood gushes from the bone and muscle in his throat, and I scream as I realize what just happened.

"Jesus, Nero, you bit his head off!"

"That's where he belongs, dead, at your feet," he says in his beastly voice, then shields me behind his big wolf back, facing the other serpents.

They seem afraid of him, surprised as well, as if they never met such a werewolf before. He's the Alpha of his pack, big, scary and apparently particularly cruel. Two serpents try to attack him, but he bites one's head off while he's still in the air, while stabbing the other with claws that shoot like knives out of his huge right paw.

The pierced creature falls to the ground with gushing wounds, in which moment I think of Wolverine and his adamant claws. That's exactly how Nero's claws flashed out of his fingers.

The other serpents make to withdraw, but they bump into other wolves, their growls stirring the night. Damn, they stalked here from the woods so quietly that I didn't even sense their presence. Their fangs glint in the moonlight as they open their snouts to bite whole chunks out of the serpents' bodies.

I can't watch this. It's a massacre. I cover my ears to protect from the serpents' desperate rattles, pushing myself against the wall. I'm aware of Nero always around me, but he doesn't fight anymore. He just watches like a wolf god. Only those who make it by his soldiers, proving themselves dangerous enough, get to approach and fight him. But every time all it takes is a swift Wolverine-like claw to kill even the best serpent fighters, the whipping sound of his emerging claws cutting through the air.

I don't know how long it is until the fight is over, but I know that serpent slime trickles down my arms. Gore must be sticking to my leather outfit, as it is on my shoes, but at least I don't feel it.

When the wild movement does settle down and I can make some sense of the chaos, the first thing I see is Paola Valdez's rigid face with open eyes, a pool of blood under her head.

"God, she's bleeding heavily," I shriek, hurrying over. But there's nothing I can do, she's gone, her big dark eyes fixed on the last image she saw before she fell—Nero in his wolf form.

"She always wanted to see me shift. Too bad it had to be this way." There's sadness and regret behind Nero's words.

He helps me up to my feet, and I look at the serpent bits and pieces scattered around, slime splashed over the tiles. He says something to me, but I no longer understand. Overwhelmed, I faint in his arms.

Nero

IT'S BEEN DAYS SINCE the massacre at Theodore's manor. I made sure there's no trace left of it, as if it never happened, but it stayed in Princess's mind and heart, and I'm afraid it changed her forever. I've been trying to talk to her ever since, but she's been avoiding me, and my impatience is turning into despair.

I promised I would give her space, but these days have felt like an eternity, and I'm worried she's learning to live without me. I can't let that happen, and since she won't return my calls I drive like a mad man to her father's manor, caution he damned.

The butler opens the door. After a stiff greeting I sidestep him, stalking directly to the drawing room, to the tunnel that leads to her room. But I run into her father, sitting in his wheelchair right in front of the fireplace, blocking my way. He's a forbidding presence with a lot of energy despite his handicap.

"If you're here to see Princess, forget it," he decrees.

"Why?"

"Why? You're a playboy that only uses women. I won't let you do to my daughter what you did to Paola Valdez."

I won't take any more of this shit. I fought an army of serpents for this woman, driving them away from Darkwood Falls. I won't let anything come between us again, no matter what.

"Listen, Lord Skye, and listen carefully because I'm only going to say this once. There's nothing you or anyone can do to keep me away from Princess. Theodore Fritz tried to come between us, and look what happened to him."

"That's right. What happened to him?" He doesn't know, because my team cleaned the whole scene. Officially, Lord Theodore Fritz disappeared without a trace and nobody knows why. But I might as well give Princess's father a hint.

"He had to leave Darkwood Falls," I say darkly. "As will anyone else who will ever dare stand between Princess and me again."

"Are you threatening me?"

"No, I would never hurt Princess like that, threatening her family. You're as sacred to me as you are to her. I just want you to know that what I feel for her is real love, Lord Skye. I know you don't trust me, but believe me when I say no one will ever feel about Princess the way I do. I'm not here to ask you for her hand in marriage. I'm going to marry her with or without your blessing, and I will protect her. I will drain my own blood to the last drop if it means keeping her safe. But I'll never leave her, no matter what, and there's nothing you can do about that."

Charles Skye is speechless. I can sense he wants to talk with me some more, but I'm burning to see Princess, so this conversation will have to wait. I walk around him to the fireplace, opening the tunnel, and he doesn't try to stop me.

I walk into Princess' room without knocking, too desperate to see her, and find her naked, just gotten out of the shower. She has a towel wrapped around her body, and her phone in her hand. I stalk to her and take her in my arms, crushing her to me, and she doesn't try to resist it. Her eyes roam all over my face as if she's starved for the sight of me, but there's more to the look in her eyes. It seems she's just gotten some shocking news.

"I just talked to Janine. She said you sent one of your brothers to protect her, and she doesn't understand why. He's acting weird, not letting her go anywhere without him."

"The serpent we kept alive to tell us about his masters' plans said the serpent shifters will try to impregnate more women of Darkwood Falls. Luckily most of them live here, in town, which we've got secured, but Janine is a business woman, always on the move. She's exposed, and she'd make one hell of a catch for the serpents. She needs protection. I got a bodyguard for your mother as well, I hope you don't mind."

"Of course I don't. But for Janine you sent Conan. I mean really, he's a humongous beast. He'll scare all her suitors away."

"Which is probably for the better. But I didn't come here to talk about Janine and her new bodyguard. I'm here for you." I press her to my body. "How long are you going to keep punishing me, Princess? Why prolong this pain, why keep rejecting me?"

Her caramel eyes are bright with need and longing. I tower over her, touching her sweet face. By God, the simple feel of her skin on mine is enough to set me on fire.

"I'm not rejecting you," she whispers, wedging her palms between us to create some distance. I can sense it's because she can't control herself around me. I scent her creaming pussy, her hormones running wild, she wants me as much as I want her.

"It's just that, it's not easy for me after I saw you kill those creatures like that. You're a killing machine."

"And I never denied that. Princess, I never lied to you. I couldn't do that even if I wanted to. I always answered all your questions in honesty, even though I might have avoided the complete truth here and there, simply because I wanted to protect you."

Her face changes to show the pain she's accumulated. God, I don't want to imagine what she's been going through these past days, locked in this room and trying to cope with everything that happened.

"Protect me? The same way that Conan now protects Janine, and that other guy protects my mother? That's not only protection, Nero, it's also a new form of confinement."

I tighten my powerful arms around her, forcing her to stay, not giving her any more space.

"Even if that protection weren't necessary, Princess, I'd still be constantly around you, stalking you. You will never be free of me. My love for you is deep, but also obsessive, possessive, compulsive. You'd have to kill me to get rid of me. What happened at Theodore's, I'd do it all over again if I had to, I'd bite anyone's head off if they ever threatened you like that."

"Theodore," she breathes, her eyes lost, and I know she's replaying what happened in her mind. "How could he defy you like that, I can't stop wondering. He wasn't a stupid man. I mean, you've been an Alpha for many centuries, he should have expected you'd be prepared for the situation."

"He didn't expect that I would appear at all. And he didn't expect that I knew the serpents were coming from the underground. But I knew ever since we discovered the ancient altar of the serpent god deep in Theodore's gardens. While the two of us made love, my senses were even more heightened than usual. I heard them slithering underground, right under that altar. It's how Theodore knew for a fact you and I were having an affair. Because the serpents from the underground told him."

She keeps looking at me, as if trying to read how sincere I am. "What about Paola? I can't accept you had an affair with her for so long without her meaning anything to you. That would make you a monster. And my father would be right."

"I never said Paola didn't mean anything to me. She just didn't mean as much as you. Besides, my affair with her had a point—I knew she was in with the serpents, and I was using her to get to the serpent leader back then. The leader found out, and sent her away from the States, allegedly on business, to cut her liaison with me. That's why I had Theodore invite her to Darkwood Falls when he mentioned her. Because I knew she was related to the serpents, and she was a good lead for us."

"So much using people," she says. "You can be a villain, Nero, which is why I need distance, at least for a while. I have to think about this."

"I'm sorry, Princess, can't do. I won't spend another day away from you even if the devil himself emerges from hell and tries to come between us. Besides, you love me, too, I can feel it."

"I'm your fated mate, I'm somehow compelled to love you. It's hard to explain, but you're more like a drug than a Prince Charming."

"Really? Then tell me all you feel is this compulsion. Tell me that your love for me isn't real, it's just the mate's call, and in truth you despise me because I'm a beast and a killer."

Tears pool in her eyes as if the idea alone hurts her. She places her white hands on the sides of my face, and rises on her toes, wanting to kiss me.

"Damn it, Nero Wolf, I must be sick and twisted, but I love you so much that it hurts. I shouldn't want you the way I do, not after I witnessed your cruelty at Theodore's, and that's the main reason why I need the distance. But if you ask me what I really want deep down, then this is the naked truth—I want to be yours, I want to spend every night in the arms of my big bad wolf. And I want your cubs."

Emotion explodes in my chest. I lift her up in my arms and head with her to the bed, my cock iron hard for her.

"I'll plant my cubs inside of you, my alpha queen. And I'll start right now."

I lay her down on the bed, unwrapping the towel from her body, and pushing her legs aside, kissing her wildly. I could care less who hears us, even who catches us. But then her cell vibrates back on the vanity table where she dropped it, and then mine does, too. Both our phones vibrating can only mean it's serious. I hitch mine from my pocket. It's Conan.

'Come to Janine's hotel in the woods ASAP. You won't believe this shit.'

One look at each other is enough for Princess and me to make the decision at the same time. Conan has seen and experienced some serious amount of shit in his long life, and if he sends a text like that, then it must be huge. Janine texted Princess about the same thing.

We grab our clothes, and only ten minutes later I'm holding the door to my car for my future wife, in front of her father and the servants. I let my eyes sweep over their faces one last time as I head to the driver's side—yes, we're together now, and if anyone ever dares come between us again, I'll rip their heads off.

THE END

Enjoyed this story? Wonderful! Authors always appreciate a review, so please leave one, if you feel like it. But there's more, much more! This series continues with Conan and Janine's story in *Protected by Conan Wolf*, coming out in July, so stay tuned.
But that would be the third book of the series. If you haven't read the first one, grab it here, and enjoy it to the max :)

If you need more paranormal love to fill your time until June, enjoy the Dracula's Bloodline series (five books already out!), available on Amazon now:

Printed in Great Britain
by Amazon